THE LAST KNOWN
RESIDENCE OF
MICKEY ACUÑA

THE LAST KNOWN
RESIDENCE OF
MICKEY ACUÑA

Dagoberto Gilb

 Grove Press
New York

Published simultaneously in Canada
Printed in the United States of America

FIRST PAPERBACK EDITION

Library of Congress Cataloging-in-Publication Data

Gilb, Dagoberto.
   The last known residence of Mickey Acuña / Dagoberto Gilb.—1st ed.
   I. Title.
PS3557.I296L37   1994   813'.54—dc20   94-5090
ISBN 0-8021-3419-X (pbk.)

DESIGN BY LAURA HAMMOND HOUGH

Grove Press
841 Broadway
New York, NY 10003

Acknowledgments

My thanks to Wendy Lesser, editorial deity, and Rick DeMarinis, a friend. They both said yes. Un abrazo fuerte for Bill Timberman, there from page one, who praised, mocking any who said no. And, finally, I can't forget Orlando Garcia, who I hope is out there painting somebody's house for big bucks, who once told me, in his way, when it mattered, to write this.

I'm grateful to the Texas Institute of Letters and the University of Texas at Austin for the gift of a Dobie-Paisano Fellowship, which first let me get serious about this novel, and to the National Endowment for the Arts, for a fellowship that stood me back up.

I

Mickey said he'd checked into the Grand because he needed a place to stay cheap, and this downtown hotel seemed as good as any. But once he'd been there long enough that he almost didn't wince about the smell, he got afraid he might begin feeling *so* sorry he'd also have forgotten why and what he was doing there. So then he got scared he was going to find himself in another situation right when he didn't need it most—anything might happen with the alchies or uglies who liked yelling and fighting then spitting up or passing out on the corridor rug. Was Mickey the only one who noticed how it'd been left there unvacuumed, not to mention unwashed, for so many years that a gooey, infertile mix of desert sand and cigarette ashes and whiskey and beer and blood and God knew what else had formed a topsoil? And Mickey was being stalked constantly by those winking and much too expensive bitches, of questionable sex, swishing and waddling in and out of the conjoining rooms to copulate with men so sad that he couldn't calm his mind imagining what acts those groans and cries corresponded to. Mickey puffed up images of the future when that money came—even a portion would be good enough. It was going to come because it had to and was supposed to. He *knew* it. He believed. He had to believe because how could he not? Mickey entertained a whole range of potential fantasies. Faraway travels in jungles, on mountains, near oceans, knockout women who knew how to love. The most realistic was a car. At this loop in time even an old car and its backseat where he might sleep to save a few dollars. It didn't even need to be that particularly clean—anything that ran would do because this place, the hotel, was not an answer, definitely not what he was looking for. Not what was *necessary* for this business of his. He had to have an address so he could be reached, and this hotel was not reliable. He couldn't live on the streets, out in the open where he might have to explain himself, what he was waiting for. And why should he have to? He was no bum or wino. He needed a place to hole up *proper*. He needed to concentrate and be careful.

The YMCA advertised rooms in the newspaper. He called the phone number, asked if there were any available. The answer back was yes. He didn't jump at the idea, but it grew on him. Exercise. He'd work out with weights. He'd push himself into major shape. He'd be *ready* and at the same time he'd keep his mind off the unpleasantries and fears and doubts. It was philosophically sound: He'd be prepared for the better or the worse, mind and body.

Mickey loaded up his army duffel bag from the Grand and left without saying so long, and it was hanging off his shoulder when he pulled on one of the Y's double glass doors. Cool, blue, the sun yellow and bright, Mickey was wearing his mirror shades as he stepped in and tripped over the cane with a tip as white as the hair of the old man sitting there in the path.

Mr. Crockett was shoved up too close to the doors. Even though he could make out shapes dimly, he felt light well and he stretched his neck like a cat so sunlight would hit on his worn-out eyes—it was the last sensuous pleasure remaining in this life of his. Every day from about ten in the morning until two in the afternoon, and sometimes even longer and sometimes earlier and sometimes when there was nothing else better to do during other hours, he'd *tap tap* over to those chairs by the door, scooting up as close to them as he could for the best and most gratifying angle. And that was where he was when Mickey got there. Mr. Crockett's eyelids were closed but his transcendent expression made clear how he was lusting with the heavens. The rest of him slumped forward, the cane between his knees and stretched out in front of him.

Even with his dark glasses on, Mickey's pupils hadn't dilated fast enough from the glare of outdoors to in front of him, and so he stumbled hard.

Yet it was Mr. Crockett, startled upright, who screamed like he'd been the one damaged, even as Mickey slid across the waxed and polished floor. Mickey did regroup more quickly, leaping up to help Mr. Crockett back into his chair, saying how sorry he was, how he didn't see him. Mickey said the same thing to Oscar, the maintenance man, who'd run over—how he was real sorry, how he didn't see the old guy there—to settle Mr. Crockett down.

"Get him away from that door!" Fred, the desk clerk, yelled. Fred's eyes weren't nearly as fired up as his voice, and beyond that, nothing else gave away any overly sensitive worry about the incident.

"I didn't see that cane," Mickey apologized to Fred when he

finally reached the desk. "Honest." He even twitched remorse-fully on setting down his duffel bag, like maybe it was too soon to lighten the burden from his shoulder, that he might pay greater penance by holding it longer.

"Goddamn old man should know better, whether he sees or don't," Fred said with equal parts authority and disinterest.

This should have taken some pressure off Mickey but it didn't because a few people from inside the coffee shop—a few paces away from the front desk—had rushed out to observe while Oscar steered Mr. Crockett over to the elevator. Mr. Crockett was whimpering loud and clear about wanting only to be left alone to enjoy his sunlight in peace. It was noisy enough to make Mickey reconsider. Mickey wanted anonymity, not publicity, privacy, not spectacle.

"You guys got rooms?" Mickey asked, turning his back, trying to ignore the stir behind him. He already knew because he'd called.

"We do," said Fred, shifting his eyes up toward Mickey for the first time. He stood up from his desk, prepared to peck at cash register keys. "With or without a bathroom?"

"What's the difference?"

Fred eased back down into his tall desk stool and drew in calmness like a smoker a cigarette. "Shitting or showering in the room by yourself, or shitting or showering down the hall with everybody else."

Mickey sighed. "Money. That's what I'm talking about."

"Without the bathroom, four dollars a day, or twenty-four by the week," Fred said like it was well known and as boring to everyone else as it was to him. "With, add one-fifty a day or nine a week."

Mickey debated it seriously. If he didn't believe he should *have to* live in this YMCA, he also didn't want the streets unless that was all that was left. This place *was* practical.

"Can my mail be sent here?" he asked.

"Comes with the room." Fred pointed over to a case of glass-windowed mailboxes. "Room key is the mail key."

Oscar had returned to stand nearby, to size up this young man: hair a little long like a marijuano or, worse, a criminal. Dressed to be on the run, in an overused white dress shirt and worn-down jeans, both of which needed washing. Boots that had to have been resoled more than once.

"What about the gym?" Mickey asked. "Can I work out? Use the weight room and pool and handball courts?"

Oscar kept his attention on Mickey as though he were trying to remember something else he knew about him.

"Your room key is good for all the athletic membership privileges," Fred said unenthusiastically, in a manner—Mickey would learn—that expressed his ordinary thoughts on the quality of people who stayed here at the YMCA. Fred had made himself comfortable for the long transaction, his new blue jeans perched on the metal stool in front of the cash register, one cowboy boot on the floor, the heel of the other hooked on the low cross member.

Oscar creased his ironed and starched gray uniform into the formica counter, waiting on Mickey's answer.

"The cheaper one," Mickey decided. He'd say he didn't have much choice. Images of sleeping under sooty bridges or out in the cold desert or even back in that nasty hotel—well, they forced the experiment here. And he still had some money. "For a day. I might stay two." Besides, he had to be where he could be reached. It was important that he be able to get mail, and that it get him, easily.

"You decide to stay the week, you can pay for it up to the fourth day," Fred said. "Get the seventh day free that way."

Mickey, offended at how Fred seemed to assume he couldn't find some better location to stay, nonetheless didn't speak out in his own defense. Fred dropped a registration card in front of him, and Mickey went ahead and filled it out as a person named M. Acuña, from New Mexico, with a previous address he made up, and then unwadded some cash withdrawn from the front of his jeans. He paid for two days.

Oscar, fulfilled, slapped the formica and began the turn away from the counter.

"Back to it," Fred said, not looking up.

Oscar walked down the hall toward his duties.

Fred's glasses rested off his ears and close to the tip of his nose. He poked, deliberately, simplemindedly, the keys of the cash register, then watched the machine print out each line of its receipt. Finally he lifted off his stool and reached toward a wall of hooks and keys and chose a room. "You leave at night and come back late," he told Mickey, "you gotta show the man here at the desk this key and he'll let you in. Elevator's right behind you. Room 412. Fourth floor." Fred collapsed and fit the glasses back into a fur-lined case clipped on a pocket of his checkered western shirt and readjusted himself to the metal stool, gazing off at nothing at all.

Mickey shouldered the duffel bag from the glossy linoleum and humped it over to the sliding elevator doors and waited patiently for them to open, trying to make it appear that he had no more on his mind than this.

Which, of course, was hard to do within all the clutter and

confusion. Once upon a time, he'd tell you, he used to pride himself on his confidence and clarity—he knew what he was doing, he knew where he was going. He'd done shit. He'd been brave in battles and he'd been mean. He'd been smart when he was right, he'd gotten smarter when he was wrong, he'd been good when he knew it was good, bad when he knew it was bad. Modesty aside, he was convinced he'd once had admirers. Important dudes who demanded respect and respected him. Women liked him. Females so incredible that he himself could hardly believe it now. So what happened? Where and when did he lose it? Or had he become so convincing that he'd even deceived himself?

No. It wasn't like that. He wasn't. And this, this was for now, until things worked out like they were going to, whether he liked it or not. He was, in lots of ways, still heroic and brave. Sure he thought he could have it all, but he'd take only what he needed. Sure he was down temporarily to a room. Number 412. A nice-enough room in his humble estimation. A bed with sheets top and bottom, stiff and tucked tight, a small yet still useful pillow. A desk, a padded chair with metal legs to go with it, a matched-decor chest of drawers. Protestant stark, it wasted nothing on gaudy, baroque trimmings or knobs. Bare white plaster walls waiting there for the imagination. A window, a fourth floor view of the border, of the West in El Paso. A thick, weighted curtain that could be closed, and a heavier, solid door that could be locked—both these activities Mickey made his first YMCA exercises.

In the shade of the curtains, Mickey found it easy to sink back into the bed for meditation on the challenges of life. He was tired, very tired. Mickey slept without taking his boots off.

*   *   *

He woke up on an unpaid-for third day after he'd checked in, and he rode the elevator down, gave up money for two full weeks, then made, he would say, a long-distance phone call about the big coin that was supposed to come to him, which, he would say, was already long overdue. He passed on the address of the YMCA so it could be sent here. Back upstairs, an elevator ride up, he slurped the cold fountain water in the hall and filled a toilet, then back in room 412, after eating candy bars, he slept again. More days passed. He paid another week in advance, checked his mail at least once every day, making sure he didn't miss anything, searching the deep long sides and top of the tiny slot that was his personal Y resident mailbox; his room key always opened the permanently oiled lock smoothly. One day he snuck outdoors and brought back loaves of bread, and little wheels of soft, cheap Laughing Cow cheese, and some fresh jalapeños. He drank a quart of water, then slept more. He was still real tired, and though safe and snug in this room 412, he remembered he was worried. He'd get over this, he told himself. As soon as that money made it here. He'd be out of this bullshit phase so fast, these weeks would seem like one bad night.

Then another day, when he'd been closed up for long enough and he was wide awake, he decided to let in some light and color, opening the curtains to the spectrum of an El Paso morning. Such a simple town of simple landscape and coloring: a brown like the earth, a blue like the sky, a white like the clouds, a little gray like the pollution. Mickey knew this Wild West town was a perfect hideout. He'd pulled off his boots by then, and he was running his dirty socks against the slippery linoleum. The city out there was so still, it seemed there were only these feet of his. It was the ideal town for an outlaw on the run.

Then someone knocked on his door.

"Yeah?" he asked nervously.

"Maid," she posed in a strong accent. "I wish to clean your room now."

The prospect frightened Mickey and caught him off guard. What did she *really* want? Once he'd told her to skip him, that he was fine, he'd let her know. He'd been clear about it and was sure she'd understood.

"They told me I have to," she explained. "I'm sorry."

"Un momentito," he told her. He realized that this time might have to come.

Mickey's eyes speeded around to make sure there wasn't some evidence. Two slices of bread on the desk, wax candy and foil cheese wrappers not in the clean trash can, an empty orange juice carton he kept water in. A rent receipt. Some loose change. A dirty white shirt, a couple of faded colored T-shirts, which he gathered up and draped on the seat of the desk chair neatly. Only then did he open the door.

"I'm sorry, pero they tole me que no matter." She smiled apologetically at him. She pushed one of those carts.

Mickey tried to smile back. He didn't care to stir up anything. Privacy, not publicity. Also, he didn't want to sit there like it was all he had to do with his life, like he wasn't busy. He picked up the clean white bath towel she'd placed on the chest of drawers. "Bueno, entonces I'll go take a shower," he told her.

She smiled cooperatively.

The shower wasn't a bad idea either—truth is he might've forgotten without the nudge. He closed his eyes in appreciation under the showerhead, opening them only to be certain that an upset voice he was hearing was not sharing this group stall with him. Afterward, as he was returning his dirty clothes to their previous locations, after he'd dried himself off with the maid's clean towel, Mickey identified the voice with the old dude in slippers and pajama bottoms, no top, standing in front of the line of sinks. He was cussing. At first Mickey thought it was on account of the shaving, the man there having a real rough go of it. But now he saw that the old-timer's old-time brush hadn't yet met any lather. The man's arms gripped the porcelain basin, his face was locked into a stare-down with the mirror, until curses burst loose from the interaction. "Shit!" or "Fucking shit!" or "Goddamn fucking shit!"—each exiting his mouth like an articulated belch. They came up involuntarily unto a life of their own, without respect or disrespect to any other person's presence—in this case, Mickey's—on the same tiled floor. The man didn't seem to know or care that Mickey was nearby.

Mickey slipped back to room 412 in the same hardened socks; he didn't have another clean pair. The maid had just finished up the room and was standing beside the gray cart in the hall, right next to his door. He couldn't stop his own disease: why had it taken her so long? He gave her his wet towel first, and she gave him a clean, dry one. He asked her, as an opener, if she knew where a laundromat might be.

"Downstairs," she told him cordially. She was stuffing the used sheets into a cloth bag on her cart.

That pissed-off man, who couldn't have shaved, exited the group toilet room, and, sanding the linoleum with his slippers, echoed more bad words into the hall. Linked in observation, Mickey and the maid stood ogling in his direction. She turned her smile toward Mickey first.

"What's your name?" Mickey asked her. She was much more attractive than he'd first allowed.

"Isabel."

"Downstairs?" he asked.

"They have a washer machine and a dryer, las dos, abajo, en el primer piso, at the first floor."

She grinned even larger. This time Mickey caught on—she smiled at him just like she did at that old cussing man.

Mickey refused to be specific about why he was in El Paso, what or who he was waiting for, what the deal was, why he had to hide out, what he was afraid of if it didn't work out. He'd snap that he didn't have to be specific. But at the same time he'd drop unsubtle hints: something that he wasn't exactly happy about having done, that he was ashamed of one minute and proud of the next. While some people would think what he'd done was good, took guts and hair, was even required under the circumstances, others might pronounce it as bad or even, according to those with stronger views and no uncertainty, as criminal.

Mickey would explain to you how he was American, a U.S. citizen of Mexican parents, one from this side of the río, one from the other, both with families that were on this land only after the indios, many years before his people taught those cowboys to ride horses and be cowboys. Mickey'd tell you he was from the New Mexico Territory and the desert, from the badlands, a canyon just like the ones you saw in cowboy movies for outlaws when they rode away, an encampment known only through the inside. He'd tell you he was a wanderer, a womanizer. Mickey'd tell you various stories about what he did in Califas, or on the West Coast, or in the big city—names he used interchangeably for where he'd been. He'd say he went there to soak up the city lights, to shake out some meaning and purpose to his life where money was fat, to score high numbers, to make sloppy love lots of times. He'd insist he *did it,* and he'd leave the length and width to your imagination.

And so who would have thought that an open door at the Y would become a memorable event for him? But after sleeping it off for all those days, so comfortable in his room 412 with those curtains closed, opening a door was a little like crossing a border. Stimulating and surprising and curious and risky. Not that there was too much to see in the halls of the YMCA. Waxed linoleum floor, one door across closed, another open. Every once in a while, though, someone would pass by. An old person mostly, a bandage around something, or blotchy skin, thin white hair. And mostly someone who didn't look back over. Mickey made sandwiches with the last slices of bread and wedges of cheese. He clicked on a radio and dialed around and left it on a ball game. Ball games could always be counted on. He made calculations with his remaining funds. He was good at poverty. He was proud of his ability to survive. Every day he proved his ability. Eating had its costs, eating had its obligations, and Mickey had his principles. He'd say the need was like the one for a woman. Sure he needed a woman, and he needed food too, but if he had to go hungry, had to sacrifice, he wouldn't get in a panic—it never worked well that way. Well, maybe he would splurge and go out to dinner that night. And maybe he'd meet a pretty woman too.

He'd found a cowboy novel stashed in a desk drawer. Mickey was no reader, and he'd never have sought it out on his own. Somehow it was more appropriate than a Gideon Bible, and the story was even set right in this city where he was, El Paso. Thus he approached his reading respectfully, with care and deliberation. He'd dragged his desk chair around for more legroom, which offered up a cleaner angle from his open door, widening the view of the room across from his. If he rocked on the back legs a little, he could observe much of his neighbor in there, sitting on the bed in his limp boxer shorts and threadbare T-shirt, both only slightly less aged than him. Those days Mickey had whipped in and out of his room for mailbox checks downstairs, or for water in the hall, he'd seen the man lots of times dressed the same, and one time at the urinal emptying not his bladder but a juice bottle full of its contents. It was the very juice bottle on the old guy's chest of drawers, a twin of Mickey's own, and it was right next to a black-and-white TV and right between an assortment of box crackers and cookies, soft white bread, and amber medicine jars. The bottle was a quarter full when the old man's hand reached over for it, rested it between his legs, then returned it, more full of liquid than before. Not to say it wasn't practical to have such a bottle in your room when you didn't have a personal toilet. It was just added detail—like when Mickey first settled into the room he heard what he figured out to be this same old guy farting. Not once in a while, but all the time, day and night. That time he was dumping his juice in the urinal, he farted a couple times then. Walking down the hall he farted. Sitting in the room, door open, he farted. Door shut, TV on, which it mostly was, he was in there farting. Asleep he snored and farted. All of which could be heard whether Mickey's door was open or closed. At the beginning Mickey's sentiments ranged between disgust and humor, but seeing that half-filled piss bottle next to food, Mickey realized that this old guy, who he couldn't remember seeing in a different wardrobe any of the other days, also hadn't gone out of that room for anything but his water, or to pour it, or to relieve himself in the other direction.

Mickey had his reactions and opinions, and—based, of course, on the fact that he'd been around—he'd say that farting at will, pissing in a bottle, sitting in your underwear nosing the tube, these, with no other cares in the world, might not be so bad in the proper light. And, unlike the Grand, there were no assholes to bother you, since they were, he'd tell you knowledgeably, the greatest source of all human suffering. Though at the Y there wasn't a woman in sight either, which didn't seem such a good thing, even for old age. So, even allowing that this might be some late stage of development, a life reduced to such simplicity, it didn't really make Mickey feel a whole lot happier.

Maybe it was because of that western novel he'd been reading, where rock-hard Jake spurred his sorrel around chasing the Apaches who'd stolen off with his unflawed vision of love in body and spirit, a rich and beautiful Mexican woman named Consuela—not spelled *Consuelo* like people in Mexico commonly and on this side too named their daughters, beautiful or not— whose father wasn't as stolid in his manliness as Jake was. Anyway, the effect of the book, as Mickey broke out of the double doors of the Y, as he chanced coming out of hiding for a walk in the air, was that his eyes were on the Old West: Those Paseños in the cowboy hats looked like the real thing to him, and the paved streets and poured sidewalks took on a much more recent occupation, like an affectation, a clean shirt for Sunday, a sprucing-up despite all the dirt stain under the nails, when the boots had been shined many times instead of being replaced. The mountains on either side of the river, like certain kinds of haircuts, gave a lot of it away—raw brown, bare of civilization, their vegetation thorny and hard. Beer bottles shattered at the edges of the sidewalks and in the gutters, glittering the dirt alleys, colored an attitude that held the territory. Mickey didn't hear any hooves but felt they'd come beating up any minute. Nothing attached to the soil seemed bolted on. Not this old asphalt with all its cracks that these modern cars used, even less so the squat buildings thrown up without any attempt to be more than what they were—four walls, brick mortar, glass, enclosures for the necessities of a trader's commerce. They could not cover all that loose dust underneath, which above ground blew into the eyes to brand its reality. Mickey's mind saw lots of animals—horses, mules, donkeys—and not the automobiles or trucks or buses. As honest as bleached blond hair on a dark Mexican woman, El Paso's truth was not beauty-parlored well enough, couldn't even be ignored completely by driving on the concrete overpasses or the many-laned highway at its center, though maybe enough for those whose foot pressed hard into their Americanized dreams.

Mickey stopped at the San Jacinto Plaza, which was a peaceful place to rest despite the whiny blow of buses and hollow thud of jackhammers surrounding it, despite the harsh voice of God communing through the inspired, head-shaking man in a white guayabera on stage who pounded out Old Testament fear and wrath. Mickey ignored these warnings and brushed off a spot on the iron bench, the relief on it of cherubic English farmers sowing, then reaping, under a pleasant sun—cotton and chile grew by the river, and the wind now had soured even more. Near Mickey a wino, clods of dust clinging to his matted hair, his beard streaked gray and tangled, stretched out on his linen of cardboard and newspaper, teddy-bearing a very old and wrinkled brown paper sack, and battled to tuck himself in. He muttered to himself and everyone else about the difficulty of that until the bulls showed up to spare him his complaints, one of them ending a striped blue-gray pant leg on the bench and leaning both forearms onto his knee, shoulders still square, directing him to a bedroom somewhere else. The wino landed on the floppy soles of his shoes and scraped them across one of the cement paths slicing through the plaza. God's voice had stilled while his brown-skinned angels, these young, sweet-eyed girls in white matching chiffon dresses, passed Mickey the literature about eternal damnation and hell.

Merciful angels. What Mickey needed were more mature angels to cheer him up. He looked around. A group of gray-haired locals with straw western hats made in Mexico like themselves sat over there peacefully, wordless, in dull though neat and cared-for clothes, not too far from a bench where their Anglo counter-parts—theirs were new beige Stetsons—found the time to share words with a black tramp about Jim Crow laws and those times past. Where chopping through were the hurried secretaries in their high heels and sticky hairdos, and businessmen in sports coats and pressed slacks and those snappy briefcases. And beyond them, where women with black hair and brown hair and even red hair, those women who cleaned the rich people's houses, waited at a wooden bus-stop bench. Where Mickey saw one woman, one young woman whose hair wasn't red, it was dark copper, and it was so pretty, mercilessly pretty, devilishly beautiful.

The way Mickey told this one was that he first had to slip in closer to her, close enough to see how exactly she suited the picture of the woman just for him, close enough to make certain she was no apparition. Among the maids, she didn't wear a uniform. She was simply there for him, a message of hope from the gentle God Mickey remembered to love whenever his heart beat so excitedly.

Mickey walked right up to her, in front of all of them, two benches lined and loaded with chubby middle-aged ladies—except her, of course—waiting on the red bus home to Juárez.

"Con su permiso," Mickey said with his best manners, "but

may I have a few moments with you to introduce myself?'' His announcement startled all the women on the benches. Mickey, too, as a matter of fact, even though once upon a time he was sure he was good at these things. The less-mature ladies wanted to check him out real well before they giggled into their hands, while the two more elderly women next to Mickey's Consuela tried to be more discreet, holding their chins and eyes down as though they weren't so actively curious.

"Maybe I could walk you home," he said, suddenly self-conscious and self-critical. Was he too direct, acting like he was in a bar? Or maybe too sappy, like he was in a church? At some moments he did feel he was a bum, and she was laughing at him. "If you don't mind the long walk across?"

One of the ladies beside her gave some eye and head movement and a few words Mickey could hear—"Talk to him."

And then she got up. And Mickey was confirmed in his belief in the goodness of this world. He felt true and honest, so satisfied he was sure this was an example of how everything else might fall into place too.

Together they strolled away from the bus benches. Mickey, nervous, struggled to work past first lines. Lately he'd been feeling unskilled in some things; he was also reminded, fumbling in a pants pocket, that he was on the starvation plan and possessed only a few dollars and assorted bits of change. He was virtually broke.

"Mickey Acuña," he said, reaching out his hand. She said her name was Ema Quintero. They shook hands tenderly, like kids. Or maybe just like Cowboy Jake did at the beginning with his lovely Consuela. The way Mickey would tell it, it was love for both of them.

* * *

The two of them turned onto El Paso Street and continued to exchange the basics with each other about what each liked to do—music, dancing, movies, eating—and Mickey lobbed the usual to win her through accounts of his wild days in California, which everybody who'd never lived anywhere else but Juárez especially wanted to hear about, even if it were bullshit. He seemed to succeed at making an impression on her that he was ready to settle down and find the right occupation since he'd already experienced so much, the right place to live since he'd been so many places, and the right woman since he had, he more than hinted, sowed so many seeds.

Mickey was good, good enough to convince himself, and so his mind narrated the story and description. With Ema at his side—sometimes he rested his hand, gentlemanly, on the small of her back as they walked—El Paso Street, where he'd spent some dive evenings at the Grand, was picturesque, a setting from that western novel. Or better yet a movie. It was an old days street where walking started up an old days–style romance. Here they were, this young couple. Mickey, down on his luck, in danger, suffering through his hard times, but ready to reform. Ema, a poor girl born on the poor side of the river. And the two of them walking forward, through the town of old, passing dark-lit bars without stools, poolrooms whose clicking never stopped, pawnshops advertising themselves with blaring norteña sound, all-night restaurants featuring everyday menudo, champurrado, or café con leche, and used-clothes stores where plump, faceless, and stooped-over women sorted and sorted through the crumpled piles, searching, their kids and grandkids running into each other everywhere and all around them, never quiet, in a high pitch of innocent happiness. And look: The colors were village Mexican—black, red, green, blue, yellow, as bright and uncomplicated as a thin crayon box, as true love. The old street, the architecture on it as cowboy western as a John Wayne set, jumped to life with so many human mysteries—cowboy hats, baseball caps, bonnets, scarves, and watchmans, boots and sandals, jeans and long skirts and khakis and shawls. And the young couple, in love, drenched with this joy of being alive, walking hand in hand like nobody ever had before.

So what if it were only Mickey's view, his lonely delusion, his crush, his infatuation? He didn't believe that, and it worked just the same as mutual love anyway. What man wouldn't love Ema's hair, and even if it were dyed that color, why question her? Who wouldn't love her eyes, wouldn't want to kiss her skin? They were together, walking, it was undeniable evidence, and like a first date, Mickey paid the bridge toll.

They paced side by side, up then down the concrete international bridge, over the river whose banks were cement, where young boys, like skid marks against its gray embankments, screamed for pennies or pesos or better yet pesetas, while their sisters on the walkways pleaded, supplicant and sad, for the same coins, wearing clothes and faces and arms that reached out, whose chapped, cupped palms were no less blackened and unwashed than their brothers below them.

Avenida Juárez, the main tourist street in the city, was hollering with hawkers and vendors. Mickey and Ema didn't spend too much time with them or their blankets or paintings or jewelry or ceramics or tacos or licuadas—Ema worried so much about what the time was that Mickey, relieved, understood he didn't even have to offer to take her to the Kentucky Club for a drink or to Villa Española for steak tampiqueño, and so he gambled for the good impression, he bluffed, asked if she wanted to go—and scored. They compared los discos as they passed them—which were the best for drinks, which for dancing—and Mickey learned that she hadn't been to any of them. She could say only what she'd heard. She was not a fast American girl, looking for the quick boyfriend, he would say. She was real, he would say.

Sure of himself, Mickey wanted to show off. When they came upon the blind, legless singer playing this giant guitar, howling out his verses of love and bravery, he insisted they listen. He clinked half his coins into the poor man's rusted coffee can. The singer sang more heartily in gratitude, and Mickey's arm went around Ema's waist. He gave dimes to the barefoot and shirtless brother and sister who approached them with the moping faces and weak voices, and he pulled Ema tight next to him, squeezed. He gave the rest, nineteen cents, to a Tarahumara Indian woman with long, braided hair, admired openly her hand-woven pancho of so many colors, complimented her on her serene, tiny baby wrapped in a blanket like a doll. The mother's face was tan triste y sincera, so sad and sincere, he told Ema quietly, that whether he believed her story of woe or not, she deserved the money. And then Mickey kissed Ema on the lips.

Mickey felt sincere too, and he wanted Ema to know he intended to be serious about her. He asked her to go out with him tonight, or tomorrow, told her he'd take her to the nicest places, here or on the other side if she could, anywhere she wanted. She looked up at him with those eyes whose beauty was matched only by her hair, like a sunset, and she blushed. Mickey was so hopeful!

The couple turned off this main street right after 16 de Septiembre, and walked, this way and that, a few blocks more. Ema worried about Mickey going to her home, but he told her he didn't mind where she lived, missing the point of her concern. They finally stopped at a small, nameless calle so narrow that the cars parked there—not many—dripped oil on the sidewalk so that moving ones could fit down the middle. It was a paved street, though with brown, dusty potholes that had been sinking for many years. The houses on the block were short and very small, built close together. Each had a cemented patio, about as wide as the sidewalk, and most were enclosed with decorative wrought-iron fences, some painted pink or baby blue, most black. It probably was a quality development out in the suburbs not that many years ago. Ema's house was originally painted white, but had become shady, like muddy desert sand. The plaster under it seemed about as solid. Once plants decorated the inside of the pots on the patio. In a couple of them a dried vine or stump survived, while what remained in the others was parched dirt, cracked like broken stone.

Mickey kissed Ema outside her house. Such a kiss! He could *tell you* about this kiss. It was like no other. It was body and soul, almost better than making love. Maybe, he'd say, it was better.

Ema's mother yelled. She was mad.

Mickey waited, still content, on the other side of the iron gate for Ema to come back, or to invite him in. He would save her from here. He would take her away. He knew how some people thought. How this was a beautiful little Mexican neighborhood, postcard quaint. It was easy for rich people to romanticize someone else's poverty, to make colorful the bottle caps in the street, or a banged-up '58 Ford pickup with only a windshield, the piles of bald tires and rusted chrome bumpers in the front yard of Ema's neighbor's, to forget that the squealing laughter of those dusty, barefoot children running past was only a fragment of their ongoing lives, a tourist's snapshot of the culture. Then just as suddenly Mickey became mad at himself for feeling the opposite, for owning presumptions, for having an opinion at all, for judging one way or another, him or her or them or them. Mickey was tired of himself, was worried. Mickey loved Ema, and Ema loved Mickey.

He was sure of it. He was confused. Even if he could persuade Ema, anyone, how he used to be or how it would be, he still was broke.

Mickey didn't have to pause on that too long. Behind him Ema and her mother were arguing beneath the rounded arch of the front door, which had opened. Her mother did the majority of the loud talking, and it was often with the word no, a syllable that traveled, unobstructed, clearly, into the path of his hearing. Ema looked over at him one brief time, forlorn, as her mother blasted her. And then the door closed, firm and secure.

Mickey reconsidered. This world was also cruel and mean. People cared so little for each other. The greedy and vicious were lionized, the vain and gluttonous and pompous were emulated. On the other hand, Mickey did agree with Ema's mother. He was the wrong guy. He was worthless. He was bad. He lived in a YMCA. He was broke. He was dangerous. He was a womanizer. He couldn't be trusted. He was unstable, wild, an outlaw. He was wrong for her, and she was too naïve. It was a good thing Ema had a mother like her.

Mickey moved along. Right through the uniformed school-kids' band marching around the statue of Benito Juárez—the brass was harsh and off-key, and, as if they were weapons, only boys could play the tinny drums. Like Mickey, they paraded among the grossly amputated mulberry trees, the trunks on them painted hospital white, past the viejitos sitting there on the cement base of Benito, attentive, patriotic, past clots of pigeons.

Mickey went on over to Calle Mariscal, where the putas shouldered into doorways outside or sat on the stools inside. Mickey visited La Virgínia not for the women but because Ginny's was more like a bar, with booths and tables, paper chandeliers. Besides, he didn't have coin for anything other than a drink, two in Juárez, so even if there were an inclination . . . which was unlikely since Mickey, despite it all, thought the whores were too ugly and too old for a young, healthy dude like himself, who didn't have to pay for it anyway.

He really did want to be alone, and he was for almost two minutes. He'd ordered a bourbon and water and put it away, thirsty. The glass was refilled, which left him with only the smallest kind of change. He'd intended to milk this drink patiently, but a chunky woman, not so very great looking in several aspects, sat beside him.

"Buy me a drink?" she asked.

"I can't today," he said.

She nodded for one anyway, and the bartender skimmed it across to her. "Come on," she squinted suggestively. "Let's do something." She grabbed between his legs, at his crotch, to make her meaning clear. Mickey didn't resist. "You like it?" She stroked him.

"Gratis?" he asked. His desires contradicted one another— his romantic mind was still holding out for Ema.

She laughed. "Para tí, con mi descuento, un discount pa' *big* Chicanos." She used English to be cool.

"You don't get enough either, huh?" he asked rhetorically.

"Yes," she said, not really understanding what he said in English. She smiled intimately, playing her eyes. She pressed her hips closer to him on her stool, worked at loosening his pants, and reached inside. "Yes?"

The bartender, watching at the corner of an eye, dried shot glasses.

"I'll be right back," Mickey told her.

Back at the Y, in room 412, Mickey still felt the puta's hand on him. She had gripped more than what was inside his pants. Mickey liked to brag about how he used to be, about women. But he wasn't sure about them anymore either, couldn't distinguish their truth from their fantasy. His stories were as substantial and lasting as broken dreams.

It was dark in the room. Black and yellow. There would be no Ema for him. Or would there be? Story. What would he say? What would be true?

Mickey thought of a girl. He'd known her for three months. She was small, delicate, and smart enough to run a corner grocery store they both worked at—Mickey stocked shelves, swept, mopped—during the hours the owner couldn't. She was only a few years older than him. She was not very pretty, and he wasn't interested in her because of that, so he pretended he didn't see how big her eyes were around him, how well she listened to anything he said. He'd say anything, tell her anything. She'd listen. He didn't talk about her, didn't ask about her. He didn't care. Then one day she told him she was quitting the job, moving, and getting married. Mickey had no idea she even knew another guy. It'd never even occurred to him to ask. She'd given him this information sadly, like she might cry, since it would be once and for all over for her and Mickey. She also left an opening for him. A day or two later she brought in her fiancé and introduced him. He was not handsome. He worked as a mechanic at a gas station. Mickey felt sorry for her because she didn't love him. The next day Mickey kissed her. He kissed her and kissed her and soon he ran his hands all over her, hers over him. She was in shock, and she was happy because she loved and wanted Mickey. But he didn't love her, he didn't even like her. When she said good-bye days later, he couldn't look her in the eyes.

He would say he did love her. That he'd lied to himself and to her. He was positive about this now because, alone, he missed her and only her. He wanted to love her. He was so sorry. How could he know how rare love was? Sleepless, Mickey dwelled on her, this girl he didn't know very well or for very long, who probably didn't even remember him, dwelled on how he missed her more than anyone he could think of. On how sorry he was. On how he wished he could call her and apologize and tell her this true story. He imagined how happy she might have been if he had told her he loved her, how simple it might've been. He could almost feel her body next to him. Her breasts, her waist, her hips. She really was beautiful, his memory shouted at him now, and he was just stupid, because now he was at this YMCA, in room 412, with the yellow curtains closed, the morning a brown, shitty muck of light, the farting old man across the hall roostering out the daybreak, a western wind blowing so strong nothing loose dared to be left standing.

II

Only at night, late, when everyone else was snoring away, did Mickey let on, even if only in the privacy of his own mind, that he was not so brave or sure of what would happen. Though he kept the curtains drawn all the time, locked himself in with his sliced bread and soft cheese and water—no natural source of light penetrated the halls when he wandered out for the toilet either—he was certain his doubts and fears had something to do with the hour, with those dreams of the other residents rolling under the doors and into the halls like an unseen smoke in the dark, the viral ones reproducing geometrically in his psychic cells. The fear terrorized him with cruelty, sometimes choking his chest so he almost couldn't breathe. His heart would pound until all he could hear was the muscle pulsing, the valves sloshing open and shut, so frantic that it would not, could not, go on. It made him hot, smothered him like several wool blankets—with more weight than that. Like earth. Like heated desert soil, shovelful after shovelful, enclosing him until he'd become a womb, blackening until his body was reduced to almost an idea, a faint silhouette, without top or bottom, high low, left right. He heard one memorable sound, either from within his chest or from within his mind, he couldn't be sure. It was a click. Click after click. What was it? The nearest he could come—reading his Bible again, that western again—was the hammer of a cocked gun bouncing around a rocky, echoing canyon as a hero, or a bad guy, rode in, bobcat-sensitive to this noise. His hearing was so sharp, so keen to stalking, that the mind would approach it, and approach so closely it could almost see the great BANG about to shriek out, almost feel whatever it hit burst into jagged bits, and then expand as the bits blew out and became a larger and larger ball barely clinging together. Until what? Mickey didn't know. He couldn't follow it that far, couldn't keep up. Neither could he determine if the explosion was inside him or just so near he could feel its impact.

He'd get out of the bed and do push-ups and sit-ups. He'd keep the room dark, wouldn't turn on the lamp by the desk. He'd tell himself to relax, not to panic. He'd watch his inhale weave in, pass in front of his eyes—a bubble of wind shifting through an arroyo—then return as an exhale. Or sometimes he'd stay in the bed and first imagine his breath as a pinprick, a dot, going this way and that, while his mind became a TV camera zooming in for a close-up of the action, and the dot got bigger, became a ball of some kind, a ball in play. He focused. It was a ball game, it didn't matter which, and there this guy was, a star, the star. It was a game like basketball, or volleyball, or even tennis—it was a game—the ball going back and forth, hypnotically—and he'd compete, battle, score and score, play heroic and miraculous defense even, move after move, but only because that was how he was, naturally, unconsciously. Mickey'd follow the ball with his mind, back forth back forth, follow the power drives of his hero player, run them over and over again, in still action, in slow mo, in real time. Mickey'd run through this, and if it worked, he might fall back asleep. It was the only thing that worked for him.

*   *   *

The weighted yellow curtain the only color in the unlit, dark room, the sliding aluminum window behind it sealing in what seemed methodical silence, his back muscles tensed on the stuffing of cotton and above the web of wire hooked into a welded frame of angle iron by taut, flexing springs. Mickey wanted to sleep and to not be awake *thinking* and being scared and punchy—Why couldn't he just fuck it and leave? Why couldn't this just be finished?—when he heard a sound rhythmically building from the room next door. He listened carefully. It was a familiar, human rhythm and it was beside him, a plastered wall only disguising the proximity. It was heavy with breath, and the metal of a bed like the one Mickey was on nicked and punched the wall, its coils stretched and squealed. Right next door Mickey's neighbor was doing it solo, relieving his pressures, humping and riding his pad of cotton with an aching wong and throbbing imagination, Mickey had to suppose, red-hot with womanflesh, with the feel of breasts and nipples and wide, accommodating hips, and in there, in the warm moist entrance of an unimaginary labia and vulva, in a real vagina and not really against a sheet. It was the sound of his next-room neighbor banging hard on that mattress and panting, and Mickey was annoyed but—he had to admit it, he was old enough—sympathetic, even, once it was over, grateful for the distraction and incentive it gave him. Mickey pulled the curtain strings, unlatched the window, and let in air and other, lesser sounds. It was early one morning, he was sure of it.

Mickey considered this an important moment—like a signal to awaken himself from his own form of masturbation. Because he needed to open the curtains more. Because he needed to feel the outdoor temperature.

Mickey also needed some cash. He was really running out of

money. Sure he was safe in this Y but was it smart to wait and wait? So he'd get a job, a temporary job, any job for now. This was intelligent. Things might get more delayed and then he might seem desperate. Then he might become noticeable here and that wasn't smart. It wouldn't be right, and it'd be beneath him to live on the streets in the cold, free or not. He needed money now. He needed to be realistic.

So he pulled nails. Fat, common nails, from lumber so old it was almost true size, really two inches by four inches. Mickey didn't understand how he could be making the cowboy who hired him a dime doing this—maybe he wasn't a cowboy, just wore hat, boots, jeans, and a shirt like one, and drawled like one too. He promised two-fifty an hour, twenty dollars for the day's work. Mickey told him to just make sure he had the money at the end of his eight because that was why he was there. It was hot, the sky more white than blue and without clouds. The cowboy had Mickey behind an abandoned adobe in the middle of this field, cotton once probably because there were no creosote bushes, no cactus, just a few tall weeds. The river was somewhere right over there but too tamed to alter the impression of the desert. There was trash everywhere. Tin cans, refrigerators and stoves, washers, dryers, pipes, conduit, pistons and blocks and heads, house doors, rusted wire and rusted mesh. And this pile of lumber with nails in the middle, where Mickey was, a hammer older than Texas and about as valuable as a rock in his hand, slapping at the sharp ends until they came through the other side where he could walk them out with the claws, then *tink* them into a bucket full of other bent, hammer-chewed, worthless nails. The cowboy'd come by now and then, out from a trailer he lived in, take a look-see at how it were going, as he'd say it, and yak endlessly. Most of the time Mickey went right on messing with the hammer and some nail while the cowboy jawed, but this one time he stopped cold during a boring monologue, willing to call it a day. "Don't call me *Mexican* again!" Mickey wasn't appreciating the work very much, or the sun or the funny-tasting well water from the hose, and he wasn't in a mood for this cowboy kind of talk about Mexicans. For Mickey it was often confusing when that *Mexican* word came up with people like the cowboy because sometimes it didn't mean anything and other times a lot. It was dependent on how it was used, on the point being made, on how it was pronounced even— and from this guy the word came out like "mess-i-kin." How much would be put up with depended on how a person was feeling and Mickey wasn't feeling too swell doing such a stupid job. The cowboy was bright enough to not offer any more about "you Mexican boys" to Mickey, though he couldn't completely give up the concept for the entire day.

"They are the best women, though," the cowboy testified, his blue eyes dancing.

"That's not what the men from there say," Mickey spoke up. "They say that the light ones from this side have the pink nipples."

That got the cowboy to thinking, and got him to clear off the subject with Mickey.

The cowboy did pay cash at long day's end and he told Mickey he had some other work for him if he was interested. He wasn't, Mickey told him back. He found other employment a day later, doing construction work. The man who hired Mickey gave him his card like it was meant to be memorized: BILL KING, ROYAL REMODELLING COMPANY, and, in bold, engraved black letters, BUSSINESS CONSULTANT. The work was to make and hang small swinging doors in a pharmacy on Alabama Street. Two of them, at four dollars an hour if Mickey was good, otherwise three-fifty.

It was easy enough, got his mind off things, yet took him no time whatever and then he had nothing to do. He waited for Mr. King's Cadillac until after lunch. He waited another hour, then decided to leave because he hated standing around doing nothing even when there was nothing better to do for no money. Mickey told another worker who was there from some other company to tell Mr. King what time he left, and Mickey hoofed it to the Y, thinking he'd saved his new boss a few dollars of labor. Mickey learned he was fired when he called him that night to ask what was next.

Mickey didn't look for anything else right after that. Mickey'd say that some of the money he was owed had come through one time, and since some payment had been made, even if the rest was mostly still promise, *word,* he could be patient, feel confident, he could have hope. Better to be smart, to not fuck up or get irrational and be his own demise—"Don't whiskey up and draw too quick" was what Jake would have said in the western. That was realistic too. It was, Mickey'd say, best to stay in shape and to save what he had in case not even another payment came. Better to be prepared and ready. Better to keep his eyes open and alert since this could always go bad—there were no guarantees. He was playing, he'd say, good guys and bad guys and he wasn't going out looking like a fool even if it turned out he'd been treated like one.

So Mickey ate less to save his money. And he worked out harder, though he wasn't going out for the Olympics. His routine began with free weights. He did bench presses. Then dips between parallel bars, then some dumbbell stuff for his biceps and wrists. Then to an inclined board for sit-ups. He liked his new pattern. With more and more time in his life, he'd try to go down to the gym twice a day. Mickey was best at sit-ups. He thought he was pretty good at sit-ups.

"How many a' those you do?" yelled Charles Towne. Charles Towne didn't just *ask* about the information, he insisted on knowing because he felt it was important beyond his personal interest. He yelled only because he was on the other side of a chicken-meshed window—the weight room on the other side of double panes, in a narrow, closet-width space beside the dressing room with the lockers. Then again, maybe he yelled because he felt that was necessary too, for Charles Towne had completely stopped whatever else it was he was doing—he was a statue of attention—to ask Mickey this question, his black face all tightened up, his eyes unable to land directly on Mickey for more than an instant. Mickey shrugged, pretending to not log such details, and Charles Towne turned toward the steam room as abruptly as he'd stopped to make his analysis. Charles Towne was tall and thin, his long, carved muscles toned and veined, though nobody actually saw him do a single exercise. He was the kind of man who was remembered because in all that thinness of his, in what did not appear strong, there was still a power.

Mickey'd swim too. He was bad at it; he'd just heard it was healthy and he hated running. The old men—not Y residents, but retired, well-off men—were the champs in the water during the morning lap swim. They'd be in tiny skintights, strap on goggles, suck on a snorkel, and splash up and back, up and back, nonstop, one old guy maybe faster than another, all of them bobbing steady and in line. Mickey found one to pace him every morning. The man would be in the pool before Mickey got there and still after he left, so Mickey'd set rest times between the man's laps. The faster he went, the more rest time. Mickey'd be dripping beside the pool, dizzy, while the old dude would still be going steady.

After he'd heard the banging noise against the wall, Mickey

found himself attentive to the other amusements of his next-door neighbor. The Sarge's door open, Mickey didn't really have to eavesdrop as he spoke to his friend, a blubbery guy with a high, whining voice. Sarge, he could hear, presented himself as an informed intellectual, one comfortable offering advice and information on any matter. The Sarge's buddy heeded with manners, asked appropriate follow-up questions, and generally was awestruck by the wealth of Sarge's knowledge, as well as, Mickey learned from carefully overhearing them, by the size and plentifulness of the tortilla chips they crunched while they sought wisdom.

The Sarge and Mickey had already begun the process of meeting one another earlier, first with nodding regards in the hall on the way to or from the toilets, and more than once at the pool. Then one day the Sarge was in the lane beside him, and he was ready for some kind of unverbalized competition. The Sarge was that type of man. Mickey wasn't the kind who went out for organized athletics when he was young, not because he didn't think he was good enough, but because he didn't have time for it. The Sarge took sports and its meaning metaphorically: Winning to him was superiority, losing was failure. So when he got into the lane next to Mickey, Mickey could tell, no words exchanged, it was test time for manhood. The Sarge began his laps with Mickey's for pace. Mickey could do only five laps before he paused for extra air and a short rest, which in the world of swimmers, even on the beaches of El Paso, wasn't so great. Still, the Sarge was racing and out to beat Mickey, and Mickey could sense the man in the lane beside him, and behind him, for six laps. And after six more, when the Sarge finally hung his arms and head onto the edge of the pool, winded and tired, when he pulled out of the water pissed off at himself. Mickey, almost wiped out enough to stop a few laps sooner, had pushed on even then, only to make it seem all the more clear that he hadn't even noticed, though he'd never before swum so well.

The Sarge was still under the shower when Mickey came in for his. The Sarge was husky though shorter than Mickey, and his physique was strong overall, though not specific to any muscle group. Wet or dry, his hair was the same—straight back, tight on the skull, so thin that it showed scalp.

"I'm Sergeant Elias Saucedo," he said, introducing himself as though he weren't standing there naked and wet. "I live in the room next to yours." He reached out a darkened, oversized hand for a traditional handshake. Mickey's hand replied a little limp and awkward from under the blaze of shower water, reciprocating with only his first name. The Sarge squeezed Mickey's metabones with all the significance such things intend. "It's a pleasure to meet you," he told Mickey. This idea brought up a lot of suspect images to Mickey's mind. Why would it be a pleasure to meet him? What kind of disgusting visuals did this guy hump his mattress to? It was appalling and embarrassing and Mickey felt himself turn away, except he was standing there naked in the shower—so which way should he turn? He decided to dry off and get dressed. He'd heard the historical talk about people who stayed in YMCAs.

Sarge still kept a connection to Fort Bliss, which Mickey refused to hear about since he couldn't stand military anything— not in principle, it wasn't that in the slightest, but only because of guys like the Sarge: the proud, yessir soldier type, confident in the most cheery, can-do, rise and shine, whistle a happy tune fashion, no questions asked. And the Sarge really did go around whistling tunes. To Mickey, who was worried not just about his own circumstances but also about the condition of the entire world—it was one reason why, he'd say, he was having to live here in this YMCA—there was nothing worse than someone, a balding Sergeant someone, with lips puckered, marching around a YMCA blowing bubbly, spiced-up, muzak versions of goody-goody music. And with improv riffs. Though Mickey didn't tell the Sarge any of these opinions of his. He wouldn't be impolite about these personal details because he didn't consider it his business and he didn't want to get that intimate with the guy. Although as the Sarge and he got to know one another better—they started playing handball together—after their workouts, in the coffee shop, Mickey didn't stop himself from speaking out on the more commonplace and equally important issues.

"Fuck her," Mickey said, meaning, of course, the opposite.

The Sarge took offense. Because Mickey's taste wasn't like his? Because he'd used such vulgar language? Because Mickey didn't seem as desperate for a woman as the Sarge was? Mickey was relieved that at least the Sarge did have more than an intellectual appreciation for women.

"There's nothing wrong with her," he told Mickey objectively, turning his voice away from Lola the waitress, who they were discussing.

"Nothing much," Mickey said. "I guess beer bellies might be a turn-on to some."

"She's attractive," the Sarge assured him. "She's got spirit."

"Spirit?" Mickey laughed. "Maybe you haven't been around it in so long, you forgot about the other stuff." Admittedly, Mickey was thinking about the Sarge's passion for flat-chested mattresses.

Lola did chirp around, and Mickey liked that about her. She was the only moving presence in the YMCA coffee shop. The menu, the same morning and noon, day and night, was about as intricate as the scratched brown plastic plates it came on. Everything derived from cans, even, Mickey'd argue, the scrambled eggs, even the over-easy ones, even the white bread. Once in a while he'd try the breakfast, and always he ordered the sudsy coffee to drink while reading a newspaper someone eating there earlier would leave behind. Lola wouldn't let anyone's mug get half-empty or cool enough to sip. "Here you go, hone-ney," she'd say. That's what she called everyone, whether the words following came out in English or Spanish. One time a man tried to teach her to pronounce it right, having her repeat the syllables after him. They both laughed at her attempts until everybody there burst out laughing when it started to sound like she was saying "horny."

Most of the coffee shop customers were residents, and the regulars were those, at least on surface examination, with few actively functioning brain cells. If the patrons weren't aged, abandoned men who didn't find use for them anymore, they were younger ones who'd lost them or never developed them in the first place. They were single, widowed, or divorced, male. A female other than Lola—she didn't count, being part of the neutral decor—wasn't just rare but almost nonexistent. That might be one explanation for why so many of them looked and acted as though they were by themselves all the time. There were those who'd come down in pajamas and a robe like the coffee shop was the kitchen they grew up in or wished they had. Others may not have been wearing pajamas, but their clothes were bunched up and wrinkled and might as well have been called that. Pants might be unbuttoned at the top, held up onto the torso by design and cut, not direction. Shirts with buttons down the front, if buttoned, if buttoned correctly to the corresponding pattern of slits, might be tucked, maybe, so that they would angle off to the side. Did any of them comb their hair? Not in the morning. Or not with a comb. They came in regular, though, as bright and colorful as a black-and-white television screen.

Even in her white nurse's uniform, a slip hanging a touch too low, a wide ring, and her fourteen-carat pot stretching out the middle, her hair bobby-pinned imperfectly, Lola was a color set. Which really didn't make it any easier to understand why she appealed to a man like the Sarge—who wouldn't strike anyone as a goon, who, if not movie chic or TV slick, wasn't a slob, who, if a little dull and boring, wasn't stupid or, on the face of it, destitute, who was in most respects above average as residents went, even if he did jerk off once in a while. It was difficult to see what he could find attractive about Lola, unless it had been that long since his last sighting.

"Maybe you should go ahead and ask her out," Mickey told him, sorry he'd opened his tactless mouth.

The Sarge sniffed, made a face unmistakably chafed, finished his coffee, and took off without saying anything to Mickey about playing handball the next day.

This might have been the last conversation between the two if they'd been ordinary residents. Since the subject of women was very sensitive at the Y, being a resident also had the corollary effect, or so it seemed, of keeping women away when these men went out the front doors and into the outside world. Residents felt apologetic about their condition because nonresidents, male and female, often said "You live at the YMCA?" with their mouth twisted slightly like they'd swallowed a bug and didn't want to mention it. Residence meant something not good, something wrong. Residence was an ailment, an admission of. Residence was a shame loaded off-balance, and the internal debate was when to mention it if the opportunity to talk to a woman came up—right off, blunt and honest and unembarrassed, or casually, innocent? Or positively, as though it were an act of courage? Or should it be held on to secretly, like a married man's wife, brought up only after things had progressed far enough? Of course, all this was a hypothetical problem because, given the distracting worry about it, given the undistracted truths within the worry, given that a man needed or chose to live there, the chances of exchanging more than ten bland, unsexual—not even charged—words with a female were scarce and improbable.

So Mickey could have felt a touch bad about criticizing the Sarge's Lola fantasy. The Sarge might have taken lasting offense. Not so long ago the Sarge lost his wife and kids—particulars not too unique, Mickey found, just another sad tale about getting dumped—to some mowed and edged suburban house near San Antonio and a man with more hair in that city more lush than El Paso. Mickey didn't feel so bad for the Sarge, though. It was what had to be expected, what he considered the predictable outcome. The proof scuffed up and down the linoleum halls in overused slippers. Mickey thought the Sarge might even have been lucky to have gotten away with it so long, to have snuck out of that marriage—or been shoved, whatever—before he was reduced to the pajamas. And the Sarge didn't stay mad. As a matter of fact, the opposite. Something wheeled and flipped over in the Sarge, and he became more curious. He acted concerned about Mickey and his destiny.

Or maybe the Sarge was only being nice. Still, Mickey was suspicious. Because he knew guys like the Sarge better than that. Because, he'd say, he had lots of other things on his mind and it was hard to think straight. Because he was, he would say, counting on his last partner on the face of the earth—that mail was supposed to be coming from him—and he wasn't sure he should. The world, which Mickey had never found an easy home to adapt to, which he persistently and continually found more complicated and complex, was populated by people who were civilizations and cultures unto themselves, with languages, religions, traditions, and too many secrets. And he'd considered that, just as in some lands and during other times there were possibilities other than the One God whose Only Son and Holy Ghost, which he'd grown up with, maybe there were even larger, ancient forces out there: gods of wind and sun and moon, of earth. Like that. And or forces of destiny and fate, of blood, and maybe, in some way, everybody played out their lives in the tumult of these . . . and like that too. So besides being worried and a little confused in the specific, this was some of it too, of how Mickey was troubled: that he might be staging some old story, and he was trying to remember it as he was going along. So he kept looking for clues or messages, ciphers, so he could remember the ending before it ended. Some hint. And just as he claimed to doubt his last friend, his last link to what he was and did in his past, here was this straight and stiff military man who combed his thin long hairs straight back, the wide teeth of comb leaving Tres Mares furrows, who wanted to penetrate this mystery of Mickey. All because, it seemed, Mickey had expressed some certainty about a woman, about Lola—which is something serious in a world of the dumbstruck—and was beating the piss out of him at handball.

Like on the way to McDonald's, the Sarge's favorite place. Mickey didn't think it was only because of the discount coupons the Sarge cut out from the newspaper, it was as much the food and atmosphere. They'd drive over at around three o'clock in the afternoon for what Sarge called his big meal of the day. He liked to emphasize this to downplay the fact that he was cheap, to highlight instead a strict food regimen, as he'd call it.

The Sarge owned a four-door silver Mercury with nappy, plush navy blue interior and thick rugs. From a panel of switches on the driver's side, he made sure the windows in the car were up, no matter what the exterior weather conditions. He preferred to use the adjustable air-conditioning or heater because that shut the dirt out. The front and rear speakers balanced the sound of the radio station he tuned in on, KESY, the "easy" music station, the one for quiet listening, the same soothing rhythms heard at the dentist's office. It sure did sedate him. He'd drive left-handed, his right arm extended leisurely across the top of the bench seat, his hand so casual, so calm, as though it were practicing to be one of the deejays. The Sarge lounged behind the wheel like he was working on a tan. His driving was flawless. Cars beyond the windshield stopped and turned and coasted past, silent, hushed, miragelike, while El Paso, the brown dusty town of hard rock walls, thorny ocotillos and leathery century plants, scrolled by cozy and at ease, pacified.

Mickey was saying that he couldn't think of anything other than what he was already doing. He explained to the Sarge that yes, the way he read it, there were options in life. A person could, by using various body parts, resumé up a corporate, bureaucratic, or military ladder. Success, of course, was determined by the dexterity in the body part used or perceived to be useful by another body part of higher importance. The best people, as they were called, were those who were the most skillful at this body movement business. They were discreet and rather beautiful about it, Hollywoodlike in the glamour and illusion of doing precisely the opposite. The worst were more like slobbish, bisexual salesmen who knew the truth but not the manners, who couldn't figure out when to use what part, when to give or receive. It was much more hit-and-miss for them, and the random process had even brought a few of them into prominence and prosperity. Or else a person could get so TVed out to not notice any of this going on. There

were also the vicious, heartless, and sadistic, who concerned themselves with body parts too but used other objects and techniques
as well. Often they died trying. Those who survived had children
who were the born rich, just like the skilled or lucky ones already
mentioned. Those who wanted little to do with any of this could
join a monastery. Which probably was God's business, bureauc-
racy, or army. Others might go to jail, or mumble near an alley.
Or work for wages. Low wages because to get any higher meant
behavior like one of the above. If the person kept smiling. If the
person got hired. If there were jobs.

"You don't really mean that, do you?" the Sarge remarked.
He was spinning the wheel with his one hand. Otherwise he was
motionless. The car stopped delicately between the lines of a
parking place.

"Nah. Just a joke."

McDonald's appreciated the same music station the Sarge
did, which for Mickey had become pounding disco music screeching by then. He didn't complain, though. When someone else was
driving, and had coupons too, Mickey was smart enough to shut
up.

The Sarge ordered two Big Macs for the price of one and an
order of fries. Mickey was into healthy so he got two fish burgers,
though also two fries.

"Honestly," the Sarge went on, pursuing it.

"It's the Wild West, Sarge. Good guys and bad guys. I'm
trying to survive. How're you figuring it?"

The Sarge fixed on Mickey like he thought something might
be wrong, some miswiring of the brain. "Good guys and bad
guys," he mocked. He did not understand and left it there a few
seconds. "There's good work and bad work, good jobs and bad
jobs. It sounds to me like you need one."

"I ain't broke yet. You just envy my freedom."

"So you can starve and live at the Y, is that what you mean?"

"Don't be talking, man. Your room looks exactly like mine."

"I've got three kids to support and a divorce to settle."

"That's my point. That there you are living at the Y."

Sarge didn't get what Mickey was saying, but he wouldn't go on. Mickey really didn't know what he meant either. He had no point to make, no worked-out logic. This was exactly his problem, that somehow he could hold up the argument anyway. The difference between Mickey and the Sarge was that Mickey knew he didn't know what might happen next, while the Sarge thought he did. He really thought he did. For the Sarge, simply doing right and working hard was all that mattered in life—Mickey wanted to push the you-got-dumped button, add a little about nocturnal emissions, and Sarge would never again proselytize about control. Mickey even wondered what else there was, what the wife, for example, would contribute, since in his experience this was a source for real truth and embarrassment. On the other hand, he did admire the Sarge for his public courage, which, dumb or naïve, was tenacious.

"How's Ema?" the Sarge asked, adeptly and diplomatically taking hold of his second burger and a new, less-provocative subject. "Have you been going across to see her?"

Because he was consistently beating him at handball, without trying very hard no less, Mickey kept the Sarge polite and respectful. The Sarge measured his tolerance and credulity on the scales of wins and losses and their point spread, and he didn't like it one bit that he was having to run all over the court while Mickey stood still, not even working up a sweat. He was losing so big he felt downright inferior, damaging and stunting the Sarge's side of the conversation quite often—he was almost unable to converse. And so Mickey had to fill the gaps. Which is to say, the Sarge being so susceptible to it, that Mickey fed him bullshit that, because of this "strength" over Sarge, was allowed as plausible. Which is to say that Mickey, not so perfect himself, had created a few facts about Ema and their evolving relationship. Mickey figured that guys like the Sarge might be content alone in the night without feeling funny about it, but he couldn't. And Mickey wasn't about to let the Sarge say he hadn't found a female to make love to—he cared a lot more about winning that kind of game than handball. Mickey said he had to go on with the story for the sake of appearances. For *whose* sake he did it wasn't as clear. It was a little for a guy like the Sarge, a little to help pass boring time and use noisy words, and a little to make himself, if not better than average, not as warped as every-body else living at the Y.

"I haven't been across for a week," Mickey said.

"I never go over there anymore," Sarge told him. "It's not safe. It's too filthy, and practically everybody over there is a thief, envying everything about you that's American."

"You think that?"

"I do."

"Does that mean your parents are filthy pelado thieves too?"

"All my grandparents were born in Texas, both my parents were born in San Antonio, and as a matter of fact both do not think too fondly of Mexico. Those people come over here and take jobs from us. They should stay home and clean up their own country. In terms of natural resources, Mexico is one of the wealthiest on earth. All they have to do is show some discipline and strength and both our countries would prosper."

"You're a sensitive Chicano, Sarge."

"And you? You fall for some hot babe from over there and think we should open the border."

"That's how it is for us children of criminals and beggars. A complete failure to reason." Mickey'd been dipping the last of his fries in a splurt of ketchup. "Maybe if I keep eating this good clean McDonald's food, I'll straighten out and fly right. Qué no, Elias?"

Mickey closed the curtains one afternoon after their Big Mac, turned on the radio and, for culture, tried to listen to some polka from a Juárez station. After a while he found it about as relaxing as he did muzak, which at least didn't have those screaming commercials. So he admitted his corruption and dialed over to Top 40 for a while, then he could turn it off. He didn't mind this music swirling around the brain afterward as much.

Mickey wanted to get through this the easiest way. He didn't want to make any wrong moves. He concluded that, despite certain aspects, the Y was best for the time being. That if he felt and acted a little bit nervous and jumpy, at least it wasn't unusual behavior around here.

Somebody knocked on the door. The maid again. Mickey opened it without too much glancing around.

"Your name is Isabel, isn't it?" he asked.

She smiled at him. "Yes."

"Mickey," he reminded her. She wasn't really so bad looking, was close to Mickey's age, give or take a couple of years. She was even good looking. Lots better than, say, Lola. She was still smiling when right then they heard that old man across the hall, his door closed, fart. Mickey had to turn his face away from her.

"I'm late today to clean your room," she spoke up. Mickey swore that now, besides the other old man's cussing, she was smiling at him like he had the gas problem. And he was as ashamed of it as if he did.

Mickey slouched in his desk chair the whole time and

couldn't think of a single subject to talk to this Isabel about, even as she tucked in all the corners of the clean bed sheets. He knew he was troubled.

She left him a clean towel.

"Thanks," he said.

"You're welcome."

Hanging around at night with nothing else to do, Mickey began to whisper stuff to the other guys too. These weren't stories he'd talked himself into believing and had forgotten weren't true—he was trying to keep track. The first one, the first monster, a feature story on the subject of Ema, was a plain and easy to remember lie, and Mickey knew it, didn't deceive himself about it for a second.

"I see her on her back, her legs apart, bent at the knees, just right. You see the line between those round, beautiful hips? My fingers meet there, my palms on those soft-hard mounds of ass. I look higher and I see her breasts. Breasts so beautiful! You can guess what I'm talking about. I am between her knees. A woman is heaven and earth, the best of life itself. You know what I mean, right? How pleasure is pain, and this pain is such pleasure. Woman! I can touch right there if I want! Those lips are dark and moist, the flesh inside so warm and pink you wanna make it home. I can reach for it, and it feels like silk. Or is it the other way around, that silk feels like it? I can see inside too with my eyes closed, you know? But I don't want to close my eyes, I'd rather see what I touch, softly press that hard bone and fur. I want it like food and drink, like air. I take both hands up to her breasts. I slide my hands from inside that baby skin of her thighs, roll them over her hips to her stomach and waist, the skin there only a woman's.

I let my fingers feel where there is no bone, just flesh, go along the side of those breasts, and then I lift them up together. Nipples. I can't stop myself. You getting all this? You know how it is right then. She's on her back and she's letting me, she wants me. You see her face? Her lips and her eyes and lashes and her hair and I feel how much she sees me seeing her. My God, I get to touch her, look at her, have her, and I almost don't want to be inside her because then I know it will be over, but I do. I can't help myself.''

This was effective, maybe in particular because these other YMCA guys hadn't seen a woman in so long, if ever, or maybe because of Mickey. Mickey was a convincing exaggerator. Lots of dudes might believe Mickey, and not only Y residents. Since it didn't seem like Mickey to brag, it wouldn't seem like him to out-and-out lie. And Mickey, besides what he implied about women in his past, looked and sounded like a guy who would do all right with the ladies.

And so after he finished this Ema story, a vivid, out of time hush, as disturbing as a threat with a shiv, gagged any comments. Sarge, for example, didn't usually change expression during most other conversations; he'd listen with his thoughts on at least one other subject as well, his mind analyzing and categorizing as the discussion went along. But for this even his attention had been singular. He'd become contemplative.

"I'd go see her if I were you," he concluded a day or so later.

Mickey nodded his head. It wasn't that he didn't wish his bullshit weren't true.

"So why don't you?" the Sarge said, testy.

"I got no money right now."

Mickey was eating one meal every other day with the Sarge at McDonald's, though some days, for a change, at Chico's Tacos, where Mickey, aligned there with the Sarge, consumed exactly

two orders of rolled tacos. The other days he still ate the dry
salami, bread, that ''hot'' Mexican-style Laughing Cow cheese,
and a candy bar from a downstairs machine now and then. For real
hunger he'd still dive into the pool and swim until the discomfort
had passed. He'd quit going outside the building unless it was in
the Sarge's car or to walk, directly and back, to the grocery store
around the corner. He'd check the mail in his box and would at
least once, every day, ask for it again at the front desk, to make
sure. He still played handball with the Sarge, holding serve, not
working up much of a sweat through the exercise but only because
the white, black-ball-scuffed walls of the court held the heat
between them. The Sarge was desperate to win a game, let alone
a three-game set, and Mickey couldn't explain why, really, he
shouldn't have been able to. The only reason he could come up
with was that he'd get the early advantage and play the Sarge on
either side of the court, run him short then deep, up and back like
that, and the more he made the Sarge's sneakers squeak, the more
worn-out Sarge got, and the easier to run him out more. The Sarge
also had no serve Mickey couldn't control. Even the close games
were never really that close. Nevertheless, outside the court,
Mickey never gloated, not a word.

"So why don't you get a *job?*" the Sarge yapped. He was
really upset about losing the match and was pretending his anger
had nothing to do with this loss. "I can't understand you! What're
you *waiting* for?"

"You gotta be patient, Elias. Not lose control. You know,
squeeze slowly. Now I know you heard that expression before."

The Sarge glared sharply at Mickey, as though to state firmly
that not only had he heard it before, he could've invented it. "You
think like a kid. Grow up." He seemed to thrive on giving Mickey
the sincere, high school lecture. "If you like this girl, you have to

get a job. Maybe then you can get a place where you can take her sometimes. Even get a car to get her there.''

"You're talking marriage again, Elias. You know, I'm thinking you should be a shopkeeper when you grow up. 'Cuz you're definitely not the barkeep. The barkeep ducks and hides but likes the action with one eye. You'd just close the doors and go home until the gunfight at high noon got over. You probably wouldn't even ask who won. Just look and see if there were any stray bullet holes that'd messed up your glass windows or any of your pretty stuff for sale. Shit, you'd get some lonely, hungry woman to strut in your store and I bet you wouldn't hit on her. Because there you'd be married again, and you married shopkeepers don't even think those kinda dirty thoughts. Right?''

The Sarge shook his head and grimaced, the motions blended as gracefully and naturally as McDonald's muzak. "I'm trying to talk to you straight, and I know you know what I'm talking about. Who're you fooling?''

A question like that might seem good in lots of ways except that Mickey was fooling him. Mickey felt pretty sure of this anyway. Besides beating the shit out of him in handball, he was getting by, and he wasn't losing control, and, as far as he could tell, he presented an appearance of being in charge of things. Nobody suspected him, he'd say, nobody thought about what he was *really* doing at the Y, why he really waited on the mail. Nobody openly wondered too much about him or asked about his past connections and activities, why he was in El Paso. Nobody suspected his worry, how something bad could happen if things didn't go right. Mickey wished he could figure out what form exactly that might take, so he himself could be ready, but he came up with too many scenarios. Not that he didn't have an idea or two. But, then again, it could work out well. He had to be patient.

It wasn't in his control. He lifted weights. He tried to swim better, sometimes twice a day, always for as long as he could. He made himself ready.

The Sarge saw order, rewards and punishments meted out properly and fair. You do this, this happens. You do that . . . etc. Yet he'd been the one who said he'd been playing handball regularly all his life. Unless the Sarge had exaggerated. But Mickey was winning at other things too. Like ping-pong. He played at night with the guys who groaned about the medicine smell of the TV room where the senior residents clustered in front of the blurred, gray reception, where a faded tint of green light, a shade or two less than the polished floor tiles in every room and hall, squinted in from the opaque windows high above the basementlike room, where metal folding chairs—usually a full ashtray next to one, an aggressive curl of smoke worming its way upward—arced around the corner, where the wooden console inhaled so much dust that you'd swear the raspy voice coming through its speaker, its mouth dry and nose clogged, would sneeze. The younger guys might shout strong advice on what program should be shown there, and it was accepted once in a while, but no matter what video image or sound, it landed frail and corny into the high echoing ceilings of the room, so that the illusion of an outside world, the escape that was this television room's purpose, was postoperative—for the old folks.

So the younger guys adjusted their schedule to the room with the ping-pong table. It was a brighter location, with wide windows and tubes of humming fluorescent light above. In the corner a potted, plastic rubber tree plant colored some space green. While two men played, the rest, five to ten others, hooted and yawned, sat on a torn vinyl couch or a folding chair transferred from the TV room, stood or sat or sprawled out on the floor. Some of them would sneak sips from a half-pint bottle, or a tall aluminum can, in either case masked by a wrinkled brown sack. Some of them would detour outside, though not that far, maybe behind a car in the parking lot, and fire up some grifa. Some of them just stared, blankly killing time, possessed by their own questions of purpose and meaning. Unlike the many, a few saw the contests like a fan, as though ping-pong, at the Y, at night, was another sport for athlete kings.

For instance, Butch, who came to know Mickey in this room. He'd only played Mickey once but lost big time, and he never picked up the paddle with anyone again. Mickey laughed, telling everyone he'd never even played the game, not since he was a kid, and then took down two others right after Butch, then stood up against Charles Towne—Charles Towne had been considered Mr. Chingón ping-pong brother at the Y for many months. It was Mickey's hardest game, and it was tight start to finish, but he won. And he won the next and the next. He lost to no one. And thus, Mickey's reputation grew. Butch seemed to admire Mickey, and Butch hung around him.

"Charles is pissed off, you know," Butch whispered. "He don't like losing at ping-pong."

Mickey didn't know and hadn't noticed. He felt like Charles Towne might have a small social problem, but was still as readable as a kid in an ice-cream store. He thought Charles acted well disposed about each game, came prepared to win, and on losing showed his front teeth in a friendly manner. He never appeared to resent the outcome night after night after night. Besides, it was hard for Mickey to believe that anyone might take ping-pong so seriously. Although, on reflection, he had to concede how he himself did prefer returning to room 412 in the late evening with the win, enjoyed the victory celebration when his door was closed, that jubilant cheer of the crowd still fresh. On the other hand, if he were the one getting his butt whipped every night, he, as the loser, might be the first to not appreciate this satisfaction with his winning, as private and humble as he tried to carry it away. Losers, like poor people, dwell on the details, the small shifts of personality and attitude. Maybe, Mickey reconsidered, Charles Towne saw something from his end that Mickey didn't.

"Me dijo," Butch went on, "and he's been telling others también."

"Telling them what?" Mickey asked. "That he's pissed off? That he doesn't love me no more?"

"Es nomás que he's been talking a lot of pedo," Butch said, trying out what for him was a smile. "Está crazy, aquel mayate."

"So go on and tell me what he says." Mickey caught himself almost shouting to compensate for Butch's voice, which was so weak Mickey was constantly having to tell him to speak up.

Butch's grin broke free. "Ya sabes como habla el vato. Says stuff like 'That booshit, that booshit he win all the time.' " Butch looked like he might laugh out loud trying to talk like Charles Towne, and it did sound funny because their personalities were so different. "It's not lo que dice, bro. It's how."

"I get it."

It was part of living at the Y, the kind of people who lived there. One day, for example, Mickey ran into a guy carrying a portable radio in the elevator. Mickey'd swore he'd seen him before somewhere else, sometime before he started living at the Y himself, on the streets downtown, someplace, he was sure of it but he couldn't come up with where. This guy wasn't at all a hippie type, even though he had long hair, almost down to his shoulders, wore a leather fringed vest, and grandma glasses. He and Mickey were together riding up the elevator together that didn't move too fast when Mickey said "How's it going?" to make conversation. Not even that really—more just to say something instead of nothing. But instead of saying nothing back, the guy jumped, pulling the radio into his chest, thrown into a misery of panic. Maybe he'd caught Mickey's face innocently trying to re-member him, and misinterpreted. "Okay," he finally offered in reply several seconds later, and about as rapidly as the two syllables could be uttered. He squished himself into the corner of the elevator, to keep as physically distant as he couldn't mentally, and seemed to tremble. Meanwhile, Mickey'd forgotten to push the button to his floor, and when they passed it—the fourth—he said so, he said something about it. He didn't say it like it was that important to him, but the word "shit" came out in his complaint, and not even over and above his normal voice; Mickey wouldn't have said even that if the guy hadn't made him so uncomfortable. But he did say it, it was true, and the guy freaked. Not by making any noise, because he didn't move at all—he couldn't have, he was so tight to the corner. It was through the eyes that Mickey saw how he was putting him through some orgasm of terror. Then the doors split open on his floor and he dropped his radio right on the metal threshold of the elevator. Since it was made of plastic, the thing cracked because it hit at an edge, and its batteries sprayed out, flying both back inside the elevator and down the hall. A long groan racked this poor guy as he raced to grab at the batteries like they were twenty-dollar bills, afraid Mickey was going to want them forever. Mickey didn't know what he should or shouldn't do but he handed him a battery that had hit against his foot. It was snatched away just as the doors were about to close again. The guy, still trapped inside, stuck his hand between them, the lines in his face knotted, and he pushed with what looked like all his strength, but the doors would not open for him. Mickey had to punch the DOOR OPEN button to let him out.

Mickey insisted that he'd already gotten used to screwed-up people in his life, and by this time even the residents at the YMCA. Life was complex, though for Mickey that meant that if people like this pathetic guy were odd and preoccupied, they were no less so than a man who got up every morning to some alarm clock—one that was pleasant or screeching, it was the same whether he liked the sound or not—to button that top collar and snug up that tied only one way polyester or whatever fabric, then slip arms and legs into his uniform, the one that nobody recognized anymore as such, the one that went so unnoticed that different colors and different textures and different cloth was difference, a uniform where mixed pants and jacket meant "liberal," matching meant "conservative." A man like that who got up every morning to adjust these components in a full-length mirror—even the shoes—as medievally dressed as a bullfighter, couldn't, or shouldn't anyway, think himself less dazed and confused and frightened by a stranger who spoke in an elevator than some hippie-looking guy clutching a radio.

Mickey's attitude might explain why Butch, like the Sarge, got to be one of Mickey's friends there at the Y, while others, at other places during the same time, might not even know Butch was alive or approve of him if they did.

Butch kept a short, black-haired fuzz on his dark brown head. He wore the same brand of white T-shirt every day, the same brand of beige cotton chinos, the same rough-out tan cowboy boots. One of Butch's hands had to be attached to a beer, or his feet were on the way for one, or both hands shook. Butch even managed to sneak cold ones in while he was at his job inside the glass booth of a self-service gas station—a job better, to him, not only for this but, since people always complained about his voice, because of the microphone.

Butch didn't laugh. At least nobody heard him if he did. He grinned, several silver caps gleamed, his head moved silently, almost imperceptibly, and long, sundried lines wiggled onto his face. There were lots of these lines on Butch's almost black face, many more than there should have been. This could have been due to his growing up in Presidio, where the sun edged closer and swelled bigger than anywhere else in Texas. But most believed it was on account of his wife, Lydia, who'd left him. You knew her name because Butch had it tattooed, in capital blue letters, on the soft side of his left forearm, while a wounded, bloody red heart had been stained over it. Butch had a few tattoos. Black widow spiders and webs, a vulture, the Virgin. Most of them done in prison. It was hard to believe that this Butch had done anything so dangerous that he'd had to do time for it, hard to imagine this Butch as a convict for all those years. It was the only well-known fact—not any of the rest. The only reasonable theory was that it was the woman.

Unless he was at work, Butch hung with Mickey. It wasn't simple to explain what for. They didn't have much to say to each other because they each guarded their personal truths, though that wasn't unlike anybody there at the Y. They drank beer together— Butch would buy a six-pack, and Mickey quit candy bars for quarts. But while Butch seemed at home with one or two words and some need not to be alone all the time, Mickey hated too much silence.

Mickey might tell a true story, he might bullshit one. After a while, Butch had already heard the Ema one and its variations a

couple of times, so Mickey would tell him stories about old
girlfriends, real, imagined, or in between the two. Sometimes
Mickey would tell what really happened, sometimes he'd invent
details and activities that seemed more entertaining. He'd tell
about how they got away, how he left them or they left him, what
he did or didn't, what they did or didn't, how their romance
bloomed and withered.

For instance:

"I was traveling, seeing the world. I like to shake it up, which
is one of the problems I'm having right now. So anyways I get to
Albuquerque and I go to this one bar that gives out free food at
happy hour. Lots of it, too, not just nachos but slices from this
gigantic submarine sandwich and frijoles and flour tortillas. And
two for one drinks. It's a country-western nightclub and it's got
a huge dance floor and lots of tables all around and when I get there
there are already five waitresses on duty, even though there aren't
too many customers, and the canned music is from one loud-
speaker, though some cowboy-dressed guys are setting up a sound
system on a stage. I was glad to be there because it was a hot day
and it's air-conditioned and the beer tastes real good. So I'm in the
mood. I start by talking to my waitress, talking about her name on
her name tag being the same as my first girlfriend—the first girl,
I tell her, that I had sex with. She smiles and laughs and listens
because she don't have any other customers. Where I'm sitting is
in this dark, back corner of the place where nobody else would
probably sit. She tells me she got this waitress station because she's
new, just moved in from Las Cruces but even though she has to
have this station, it'll get better because she says the people who
come here tip good, though not during this shift, which she has to
do twice a week. I'm laughing at her making good-attitude talk and
tell her that she gets good tips because she looks so beautiful and

the tips come from men, right? She says, mostly, yes. And so I say, and it's because they want to have sex with you and you know that, don't you? And I say, but look, I'm sorry, but don't think that about me, I mean, don't think, well, don't think I'm gonna leave a big tip, because I won't, that I'm here because I came here for the free food and the cheap drinks. I don't mean I wouldn't want to have sex with you. I don't mean to say that either, don't mean to talk about making love to you. She does know what I'm try-ing to say because I'm really fumbling around, *really* and honest trying to talk truthfully to her about her and about me, and since it comes out funny, we laugh like friends. Pretty soon customers are coming in and we start talking about them, giggling and cracking wise, and she says she can bring me draft beer, and sometimes I use the phone to call this friend I know but he never answers. Then when it's time for her to get off I tell her to stay a while, until my friend gets home, but right away she invites me to her apartment, she says because she gets tired of being here and she says she thinks I'm trustworthy and not dangerous, and I can go ahead and call my friend from her place.

"Well, she was right because that is how I feel about her. I wouldn't think to take advantage, and I feel even more that way when we get to her apartment building, one of those ugly boxes where all the doors face the street. It's such a sad place, lonely and dumpy, old cars parked in the slots for a front-window view, laundry hanging off the wrought iron on the second floor. She's there because she wanted so much to leave where she was, in Cruces, where she said everybody knows everybody and it's so boring, she just refused to end up there, and one time she'd visited Albuquerque with a girlfriend and they had such a great time and that's why she came back. She envied me, she said, because she was a woman and couldn't wander around like I did, go to all those places I'd been and done all those things. She said she wished she could just do whatever it was that she wanted, go anywhere, she just wished a woman could be free the same way a man was free. She said she envied me and she got this look in her eyes. Like we really had known each other for a long time.

"We both got quiet then, I remember. It was getting late and my friend never did answer the phone. So I told her good-bye and thanks but if it was okay I'd drop in on her the next day, or maybe I'd see her at the bar. She knew I didn't have money for a motel and asked me where I'd go but before I answered she said I might as well spend the night, sleep there on the couch. She brought me a pink blanket and soft pillow. Something about that got to me. A pink blanket and a soft pillow. She knew I'd be leaving in a day or two, and for some reason (this was what she told me) that made her feel more, not less, safe. I kept on thinking about her when all the lights were off . . . gentle, kind thoughts, like I was her old man wanting to take care of her. So you know what happened. We spent three days together and she even missed one day of work. I could tell you about how it was but it's not what I'm telling this story for, it's not the point. The point is, the thing that happened, was how we were, how it was. It's hard to explain except that we were in love. We were in love and it had to do with that I wasn't staying, that I was leaving. And that's what did it, that's why it got the way it did. We cared about each other because we weren't going to see each other again. 'Course I knew where she lived, and I got her phone number, that sort of thing, but we both knew I wouldn't ever see her again and she wouldn't ever see me. Because I had just taken this drive (I had a car then) to Albuquerque, like I took drives to other places, and I was staying with her and then I would leave. So we did everything that could be done, because our time was so short. You get what I'm saying, right? Because then you can see how I think about her all the time. I think about how she was probably the woman I should be with even now, and I swear she thinks the same about me. I see her perfectly, all these details of us being together, so many little things about her body and her voice, how she looked when she slept, how her hair felt. I remember the plastic clock by her bed, the green light on it, the metal second hand circling.''

About the time of these stories, telling them, something else began happening to Mickey. Though it could have been because he wasn't eating so well, or because of his waiting and waiting—the mail he looked for still hadn't arrived—and worrying about the effects of the mail never coming, or because he was exercising too much and it was wearing him down. Whatever the cause, he was beginning to not even want to go outside the doors of the YMCA, or when he did—usually along with the Sarge in the Mercury, punched into that easy listening, or walking over to the grocery store by himself for food or with Butch for beer—even then he felt like he was indoors. His mind, in other words, wasn't making clear distinctions. That story he told, for example, about the girl in Albuquerque. It was, he'd say, a true story. And he was sure it was true. Except why was he *sure* of it? Didn't it mean it wasn't a hundred percent true if he had to convince himself, double-check his memory? And if *he* wasn't sure, if the truth of something was questionable even to himself . . .

Mickey wanted to assure Butch that that one *was* true, really. He wanted to tell Butch to believe him, though he had no reason to think Butch didn't believe it or any of the others he told, like the Ema one, which wasn't, not exactly, true. How would Mickey explain this? How without saying some of the other things were bullshit? And then how would he be able to prove that this story was bullshit while that was not?

Then another doubt. What about Butch? He seemed friendly enough and Mickey liked him, but then Butch was an ex-con for he didn't say how or what or why. Why believe him if he told his history? As a resident here, with a resident's glint in his eye, Butch couldn't be trusted either. If he were normal, healthy, cured, rehabilitated, why was he here? The disease was what a person came in with or acquired once there—either way, the disease fed. Worse yet, Mickey couldn't understand what difference to him it made—who believed, who didn't, what was true, what was not true. If he couldn't tell them apart, why concern himself? If they couldn't, why concern himself? And so on.

This worm wasn't just inside the brain either. There was this "winning," these games *out there*. Besides it seeming like he was still up on the big game—what he was waiting on—he was also winning at the little ones—at handball, at ping-pong—when he didn't deserve it. He couldn't be "good" at these, shouldn't be better than these others—they practiced, they cared—who wanted to be good at those things. It didn't make sense. Too much, already, didn't make sense.

All Mickey consciously wanted was for shit to move on smoothly, wanted the time to pass while he endured his wait. He worked out with weights and swam because it helped time pass, because it helped him ignore an appetite. He played handball because the Sarge wanted to. He played ping-pong because there was nothing else to do. And he told those stories that made him out the hero, as victorious as he was in handball and ping-pong. They were pretty good stories, he wouldn't deny it. Stories someone like Butch, or the Sarge, or just about any of those other guys wished were theirs. They wanted to hear Mickey.

"She was my cousin," Mickey might start. Or, "She was this rich girl, and she had straight long hair with two braids and strands of leather woven in them.'' Or, ''She was from Chihuahua, and I bought her a new pair of shoes.'' Butch paid the closest attention. Sometimes they were sitting on the planter wall outside the building's glass front doors, late at night, in the dark, and there might be one or two other guys, even once in a while the Sarge, though only for a few minutes, and they were sipping beer or smoking a joint, looking around, eyes open for someone, for something, staring down a car that passed by, or a truck or bike, or even the concrete sidewalk at their feet. Butch would talk—would whisper, which was his talk—about going to a bar, or to a strip joint, or to Juárez for both. Mickey'd say he just went, he'd just seen Ema, he was tired, he wasn't in the mood, he was broke. Maybe one of those was true—always one—but not exactly either. Still, Butch never criticized him about it. Butch accepted what Mickey said without making judgment, or so it seemed.

As his exaggerations melded more often, and always too conveniently, with the truth, Mickey began losing track, slipping. He gripped only the small, obvious facts. Number one was the money deal. Probably, he'd admit, he needed to go out there again and get another job for whatever money they'd give. A job. He needed a job. How could he get a job? A job. He couldn't. He just could not do it. How could he? he reasoned. He tried. He could never get a job. He tried. He couldn't keep a job. Nobody would give him a job. There were no jobs, nothing real. And why should he have to work those shit jobs? Cowboys and consultants. So he went on convincing himself that any day now this'd be over and he'd leave. Hang tough. He could panic, he could feel the urge, but he refused to. He was lover-boy cool and killer calm. Things would work out. He visualized another time, the future. A car he'd own. Nothing special, though not some ugly economy model. He'd drive away and this'd be over and years would've passed and nothing would be remembered of the Grand or the YMCA. The time would be forgotten, and he'd be like someone else, and it'd be like nothing unpleasant even happened to the new guy he'd have become. Or if he did remember, then *only* he would remember, and he could drop it, or even make it come out different—tell the story *his* way. . . . He could tell *this* as a story.

He'd lock that heavy door of room 412, close the curtains, snap on the light mounted on the wall above his mattress. He wouldn't separate from his jeans, but off would come the shirt and boots and socks, and Mickey'd get between the clean white YMCA sheets. He'd read the western slow. Maybe that was why it became so real to him, so much about his situation: Jake was hiding while those Apaches had the gorgeous, buxom Consuela. Jake had found a cave to watch them from. Not really a cave, but a dark, unknown hole where he could just barely fit. Jake just knew those Indians had *used* Consuela and it made him woozy to think of it. Mickey bet it also stimulated Jake, just like it did him. How could he not imagine those breasts of hers under his hands, in his mouth? When Jake opened his eyes at dawn, he found a diamondback coiled at his feet. He could not move. He could not kill it because noise echoed around those canyon rocks. He had to stay absolutely still and patient, doing nothing, while he watched his Consuela from the distance.

Mickey was often hungry. And one of the more favorable results of getting to know the Sarge was that Mickey got to eat those tortilla chips at night with him. Though there were evenings he'd pretend he wasn't in his room if the Sarge or his fat friend— his name was Philip—knocked on the door and called his name to invite him over, most of the time he did go, and gratefully. He'd drag over the chair from his room, and he and Sarge, or he and Sarge and Philip, or one night it was Butch, and not Philip, were sitting around there crunching and grinding, the Sarge's radio tuned in. They weren't saying much, not because of the eating, and certainly not because the muzak version of "Michelle" tickling the airwaves was so rhapsodic it left them speechless. It was that Butch never said much of anything, while conversation between the Sarge and Mickey had turned awkward. In the first place, the Sarge was becoming so frustrated and mad that he couldn't beat Mickey at handball that his lips had narrowed, and, secondly, the Sarge was beginning to openly disapprove of Mickey's behavior and lack of employment. And so the Sarge had become grouchy and peevish.

Mickey wasn't in a position to understand this entirely, and so he didn't fault him or the muzak either, and, grumpy or not, the Sarge did Mickey kind deeds and would probably go to heaven for them. Moreover, Mickey had already unwrapped a Big Mac with the Sarge that afternoon, and was now emptying the bag of discount tortilla chips with him this night. He appreciated this guy, Sergeant Elias Saucedo. Nevertheless, he didn't like sitting there so quiet for so long. So Mickey asked him what he thought of the old man who screamed cuss words.

"It's a disease," he told Mickey and Butch. Which, for the Sarge, was End of Discussion. The Sarge was in a rough, militaristic mood, and needed some prodding.

"Disease, huh?" Mickey asked. He snickered over at Butch sitting on the bed—slumping is really how Butch sat, shoulders low and guilty like he'd done something wrong. "Inflammation of the 'Fuck!' word," Mickey told Butch. "Screaming 'Shit!' syndrome." That caused Butch to make his caps shine. "He's pissed off about something, that's what it is."

"I read about it somewhere," Sarge said after an officious pause that meant he'd ignored Mickey adequately. "I can't remember what they call it. It has something to do with a degeneration of the nerves."

That really would have been the solemn end of this topic had that old guy across the hall not expressed his own version of degeneration right then. So all three of them started laughing—you couldn't hear Butch, but you could tell he, too, thought it was good timing. The laughter seemed to warm the Sarge's cool heart so much that Mickey, sensing an opportunity, suggested—hoping his sarcasm might scrape out a couple of the tasteless, musically dead cells in his ears—that the Sarge turn up the muzak.

But suddenly someone pounded on the door. Very hard too, because the aggressiveness of it choked their new good spirit. Which did not make the Sarge a happy person.

"Who is it?!" he barked with all his stripes.

"Open the door right now," a deep voice said. "This is the police."

There was no reason to imagine it was the police, but the Sarge jumped up. "*Who* is it?" he asked, frightened.

"Just open this door right now!" the voice on the dark side of the door hollered back. There was more pounding, a hard shaking of the locked door.

Mickey looked at Butch, Butch looked at Mickey. Neither of them had had time or reason to be worried yet, though Butch opened his eyes a little more and both his hands lodged on the can of beer, while Mickey wasn't ready to dismiss it as some kind of bad TV sitcom joke. But the Sarge leaped into both the melodramatic and the solemn, stabbing his hand into a suitcase he had on the floor to dig out a baggie full of marijuana and white cross pills. It was difficult to imagine that the Sarge was a weed smoker, impossible to imagine him using stimulants. The surprise stretched Mickey's muscles into a wide grin even as the Sarge asked him for an opinion.

"I dunno," Mickey told him, having trouble with his mouth and other motor powers, he was smiling so hard. "I really don't know, Elias."

The Sarge had already moved conclusively by the time Mickey responded, straight toward the window, which opened for him effortlessly. He shook the baggie's contents into the air and down onto the sidewalk and planter four stories below, and then let loose with the tainted baggie too. He watched a plaintive moment, split seconds, as it floated down like a bubble, and it seemed like the Sarge wanted to mourn there longer, but instead, decisive man that he was, he turned to the door.

"What's cooking?" Philip, the Sarge's fat buddy, asked. He was, by the way, a criminology major at the junior college.

The Sarge didn't spit out a word, and neither did he scowl. His head simply fell against his chest and he sat back down at his Y desk and did not make eye contact with either Mickey or Butch. The muzak was mellowing out an overly harsh Henry Mancini theme and Philip walked over to the bag of tortilla chips a little confused.

"All that Mantovani never to be appreciated again," Mickey told him. "No more energy for whistling."

"What's wrong?" Philip asked the Sarge. He took a few curled triangles in his left hand, and with his right took one from the left hand and fit it in his mouth, contemplating the Sarge's reticence. "Because I was spoofing that it was the police?" he asked with corn pieces stuck to his teeth. "What're you guys doing?'' he said suddenly, a touch suspicious, though mostly, his mouth full, contented. ''I thought you'd just know it was me,'' he told the Sarge.

The Sarge wasn't verbal as yet, but did tilt the position of his head.

''Here's some dip,'' Mickey said, handing Philip the soft plastic tub from a supermarket. ''The Sarge wanted us to celebrate, so he splurged.''

''Great,'' Philip said. ''You guys were partying, huh?''

Finally the Sarge tried out a smile from one side of his mouth. ''Where have you been keeping yourself?'' the Sarge asked him.

''I was visiting my grandmother in the Lower Valley. Hey, my grandma has this neighbor. A divorcée. She's hot. I was thinking about staying around, but she has kids, and you can't mess around at my grandma's house either. And I wouldn't exactly think she'd sneak in here with me.''

''Probably not,'' said the Sarge, sarcastic, cynical—pissed.

''Hey, listen to this,'' said Philip. ''There's this restaurant there—great rellenos—but they have different prices for Anglos. Can you believe that?''

''How do you know they do that?'' asked the Sarge. He bristled with authority.

''I ate there.''

''But how do you know they charge you more than anyone else?'' the Sarge probed.

''Because they keep two menus, with two sets of prices.''

''Bullshit,'' Mickey said.

''It's possible,'' said the Sarge. Now he got competitive.

''Bullshit,'' Mickey said. ''Stupid bullshit.''

''I think it could have happened,'' said the Sarge. He really wanted it to be true, wanted to stomp it into Mickey. ''Did you compare the menus?'' the Sarge asked Philip. He just wanted to win this minor skirmish bad.

"There was nothing to compare," Mickey interrupted, " 'cuz they didn't do that. And if there was, if there was a price difference, it'd be cheaper for the Anglos and more expensive for raza. If somebody in a restaurant around here was thinking stupid, that's the kind of stupid the thinking'd be."

"Just for the sake of argument, let's say it's possible," said the Sarge. "So what would you accept as evidence if you can't be there yourself?"

"Maybe a detail I can be sure of."

The old man across the hall cut one.

Mickey had almost become serious. "Hard to be sure of much, but you do have to decide. Like you just did."

"How do you know who to believe?"

Mickey shook his head. "That's a lot of the trouble with the world, right? Lots of people believe what's not true. Especially in places like this."

"They might be right, though."

"Might be."

"Did you see two menus?" the Sarge asked Philip.

"I didn't have to," Philip said defensively.

Mickey laughed at the Sarge. Game, set.

Butch had finished his beer, got up, and whispered about going out to get another.

The next morning, on the way to the gym together, Mickey and the Sarge were inside the elevator going down to the lobby.

"I'd never have figured you for a doper, Sarge. You're a surprising guy."

"I almost forgot to tell you," the Sarge said, ignoring that. "They're looking for someone to be a desk clerk. You should take it. You should get yourself a job."

For a second Mickey thought they were playing some more. "You need someone to score you *más mota*? I got conectas, you know."

The Sarge still wanted to ignore it.

"Never again will I think of you as Mr. Straight and Narrow. I got something on you, but I won't let on to nobody."

"I don't use myself," the Sarge said. "I just keep it around . . ."

"Keep it around? Keep it *around*? What's that *mean*?"

The Sarge, his jaw tightening, looked away sternly.

Mickey *wanted* to get off the subject, and that idea of a job welled up.

Fred was working the desk. "Is it true?" Mickey asked him. Oscar was leaning into the formica counter, examining Mickey's face, listening much too carefully.

"They're having me work an extra four hours to cover the spot," Fred said from his stool, not a nerve or muscle showing. "And I sure didn't ask for 'em."

"You think they'd hire me?"

Fred didn't respond. He didn't blink. Talking to him was a lot like talking to Butch, except when his mouth did make sounds, Fred's voice was not hard to hear—even from around the corner, in the coffee shop.

"Whadaya think?" Mickey asked him again.

"Now how the hell would I know?!" Fred meant that.

Oscar refused an opinion as well, but at least his body squirmed around definitively, and he slapped the formica.

"Back to it," Fred said.

It would be either the best choice or the worst, Mickey couldn't be sure. There was something about his working the desk that was going to make the difference. He believed that. He didn't *know,* but he believed it, really believed.

III

Mickey didn't care much for Lola's attitude. Because he couldn't see any reason he shouldn't have gotten the job. Especially considering how he was a man with such experience and skills. If anything, it was beneath him to work for such a low wage. It was one thing to take some shit job that paid cash at the end of the day, another to work for so little on a regular, everyday basis—like she did, he might have told her. Then again, it didn't really matter to him what someone like Lola thought, and what bother it caused was too small to complain about—though, on the other hand, why let it go completely.

"You think they were gonna wait for someone with a college degree in desk clerk?" he asked her. "I did hear how they needed somebody with more background in table wiping. You should apply for the next opening."

Lola didn't respond because she couldn't understand why Mickey got so agitated. Like every day, she'd been more occupied with telling Mr. Crockett to drink his soup before it turned cold. She hadn't really been paying that close attention to what she'd said to Mickey.

"Don't get such a tizzy, hone-ney," she told him warmly, though still fretting over Mr. Crockett. "I only think it's funny." She wiped up a little spill of coffee Mickey had made. "I just can't see you go talking to el grumpy Big Ears about it."

Mickey didn't know Mr. Fuller was called Big Ears yet, so he didn't have much more to add.

"Here," she said, trying to make up even better with him, "I give you some more coffee on the house."

Big Ears was the nickname of the man in charge of the Y—really the second in charge, but at least the most apparent boss, since he hired and fired and gave orders. The Sarge had told Mickey how he'd talked to Fuller, Mr. Joseph P. Fuller, about Mickey needing this job and being smart enough to do it. Told Mickey to go see this man in his office. Mickey didn't understand why the Sarge had gone to such trouble on his behalf. That was maybe because he was so distracted with foreboding about working there—worried about some yet unknown, sinister consequence of this activity. Would he be too conspicuous, too easy a target even? If he really needed a job, wouldn't it be smarter to go out and get another someplace where he didn't live? Or would it be to his advantage to be here at the Y, able to see things before they occurred, so to speak? It even pissed Mickey off that he needed this job. It should not have been. He shouldn't have had to be hanging out at some YMCA, rationing food, let alone weighing a very small money advantage he'd get as an employee for his room 412. Why, he was continually berating himself, hadn't this worked out right and appropriately? So he'd gone into Mr. Fuller's office slamming all these beforehand thoughts off the walls of his skull. He was fully prepared to not take the job if this Fuller dude had too many questions, or if he wanted too many forms filled out. Or if he didn't treat Mickey with the absolute utmost respect and regard, then fuck him and it, he didn't need no desk-clerk job.

Mr. Fuller spoke gently, reasonably, without prying or any untoward interest at all—Mr. Fuller did have big ears, his hair was thinning at the front and gray on the sides, he wore a gray suit and blue tie—and he told Mickey to go and have Fred show him how to work the cash register. Conditions that Mickey could agree to.

"Just about anybody could manage it," Mickey muttered at Lola. "You keep being nice to me, maybe I'll teach you one day."

"Whadaya think, Lolita?" asked the large, older man from Michigan sitting across the horseshoe counter from Mickey, lowering his newspaper and unlatching the glasses from his ears. "You think you could handle the big time?" He laughed way out of proportion. Lola listened to him at the side of her eyes, wiping her hands on a stained bib apron that insulated her white uniform. Lola saw things her way, even if she weren't always right. She'd been working at the Y a long time, had been around lots of weeklies like Mickey, and more than a few longtime month-to-months like the man from Michigan, and she'd learned not to accept the surface conversation, even if she never came to know what lay beneath. She watched how, every afternoon and for seven years, give or take, this man from Michigan sat at the counter—his favorite, same spot unless it was taken; he was buttoned up, whether the building was heated or cooled, in a warm, red flannel shirt—she'd counted three different versions—reading the afternoon El Paso paper, griping about it in comparison to the papers he knew in Michigan, then going on about Michigan and in Michigan and the people in Michigan, how things used to be there and how things should be here. If he were sweating, it was too hot, the heating was up too high, or the air-conditioning was worthless. If he were too cold, why couldn't they turn up the heater?

So how could anyone expect Lola to believe it wasn't the same with every one of them? There was, for another example, the new young resident sitting next to Mickey. He was a lanky, ruddy-faced man who wore a dark brown cowboy hat and went by the name of John Hooper. He was an afternoon coffee shop regular too, coming in before his swing-shift job as a truck dispatcher. A good, regular job. The Y, she heard him telling Mickey one afternoon, was the cheapest decent joint in town, and he was saving money by living here. John Hooper might have sounded sensible, respectable, even normal, but while Lola had her suspicions about him too, people like Mickey might not notice for a long time.

"The old farts can get to you, though," John Hooper said, nodding over at the man from Michigan. "Get right on your nerves. You know what I mean?"

"Getting old does not seem too pleasant," Mickey acknowledged.

"It's not just getting old. It's something about wanting to stay here. Especially those Yankees." This time he grimaced over at the man from Michigan.

"I thought you liked being here," said Mickey. "I thought you didn't mind it."

"I just use the bed, nothing more." John Hooper said that logically, intelligently. "So what're you in for?"

"I'm just broke. A bad location in time." Mickey looked at him to see if he'd gotten by with that much. "It beats hotel dives. I think so anyways."

"Lotsa guys pass through," said John Hooper. "Lotsa them are nuts, some of them are fags, some of them are perverts."

That made Mickey flinch. John Hooper didn't look either homosexual or perverted, but Mickey'd learned to take note of the words on somebody else's mind, no matter if he used them positively or negatively. "I guess as long as nobody hits on me," Mickey told John Hooper.

"They hit on me, I fuck 'em up," John Hooper snapped back, his words swinging like fists.

"You had guys hit on you?" Mickey hadn't had this problem yet, but it was an institutional reputation he'd heard about often enough.

"Nah. I wouldn't give any of 'em the chance. They know I'd fuck 'em up if they did." He touched the brim of his cowboy hat, like a salute. "Anyway, if I'm here, my door's closed. Otherwise I'm not here."

John Hooper was about as average in appearance as they came, with what seemed like average impressions and reactions. And, except for Lola, about everyone thought so, and Mickey wasn't an exception. Mickey, contrarily, did not think he himself too common. Not that he thought something was wrong with himself, but because he wasn't the usual, he wasn't confident about criticizing things other, average folks like John Hooper might. John Hooper, for instance, pushed his hat down tight and groaned, disapprovingly, when Blind Jimmy pranced into the restaurant that day, while Mickey smiled. John Hooper stalked out, and Mickey settled in. Just before he lighted out, John Hooper said, "See what I'm talking about? A buncha sickos." Mickey, by contrast, told Lola to pour him some more coffee, since he still had a few minutes before he had to turn himself over to the desk.

Blind Jimmy was as pale and thin as a fluorescent lightbulb, except for the bright red welts of pimples that rouged his cheeks. His thin yellow hair hung away from his forehead like some circus wig with countable, moplike strands, each the same length. But as he tapped in, happily, with his all-white cane, none of this, not even his rolling, bloodshot eyes looked as strange as the lacy, pink dress he was wearing. A pink dress and a pair of brown, unpolished loafers, with white socks—neatly rolled at the top—above.

The sight didn't cause Lola to smile for a second. It was a pure and gasping shock for her and she insisted on an explanation for just what it was he was doing, how come he had on a girl dress. Jimmy, even wearing a different voice, told how he wanted to be a girl, a big little girl, he wanted to be an eight-year-old little girl. Lola didn't react well to Jimmy's aspirations, and she gave him a glass of ice water. Like others around, Oscar thought it was entertaining, up until Lola dogged him to get someone in the office to call someone with influence over these disruptions. Then Jimmy started singing a song. "Swing low, sweet chariot, coming for to carry me home." He was so happy, he was so very happy. He sang with pleasure and exuberance, causing such bemusement for the man from Michigan that he folded up his newspaper and caressed it under his armpit, while Mr. Crockett rocked in his chair with a drooling concentration. Mickey considered the musical event spectacular and brilliant whether that was a little girl's voice or not. It upset only Lola, and she'd even gotten mad at Oscar for not doing more about it, even after he'd returned saying he had told Fred and how Fred didn't know what he could do and how Fred didn't want to think of anything either.

It wasn't that long, however, before a gentleman in a blue suit and with a soft drawl came for him. Jimmy, still pressed into the stool and against the coffee shop counter, by this time was about finished with another hymn, "The Whole World in His Hands," but he was stopped before he could wrap it up. He wasn't disappointed that this man had come for him, and the man admitted to believing Jimmy about wanting to be changed into a little girl, that he wanted an operation—Jimmy kept reminding him, chiming over and over—and the man said he knew, yes he knew, yes, okay, let's go, he knew. The man followed the tiny-stepped pace of Jimmy, agreeing to many promises, and it appeared that Jimmy, his naked arm linked to the suit sleeve of the man, his white cane stiff against his pink chiffon dress, sincerely trusted what he was hearing.

This was Mickey's second day at the desk.

"It makes you kinda sad, don't it?" he asked Fred.

Fred squinted his Oklahoma Indian eyes straight at him. "The boss says you screwed up some on the register yesterday," he told Mickey, matter-of-fact, dismissing what wasn't his inclination to pursue. "I'll show you once more."

"That means you don't think it's so sad, huh, Fred?"

Fred started describing the various meanings of the alphabet keys again, the ones punched before the money numbers to tell the machine what category that money was for. He went through it slowly and patiently, and not judgmentally. "You got it?"

"I got her good now, Fred, honest," Mickey said, a touch offended to have to be taught again, even if he had gotten a couple of transactions wrong the night before. "In other words, you don't think it's a sad thing to be a blind young man who wants to become a little eight-year-old girl?"

"I've seen lots of people check in and out over the years." Fred grabbed up a denim jacket and squeaked the hinges of the hip-high, swinging door. "You have any more trouble, you remember to ask about it tomorrow."

That was how it was for those, like Fred, who could just go along in life, making a go of it somehow, doing what . . . well, what they did, with enough conviction to keep going without stopping or screwing up.

Which is why Mickey envied them. Because all he really

wished for was something like a clear, unpolluted understanding. Clear? Maybe even more than that. Mickey was alert for a holy directive issued from God or His Equivalent. A bush. A special twinkle in the sky. A voicelike shaking underfoot. Anything like that. Mickey did not want messiahhood, prophethood, sainthood. Mickey was simple in this: He wanted one truth that was, at least, true. He could get healthy off that. Like aspirin for the headache, Alka-Seltzer for the stomach, socks for cold feet.

Mickey was obsessed with doubts, with indecision and inaction. Why not like Blind Jimmy, singing in the coffee shop in a pink dress wanting a sex and age change? Why not like Fred, punching in for forty or more a week unto retirement? It was, he reasoned, one or the other, a matter of pivot, not point. One accepted being taken care of, the other took care of himself. Both were true and conclusive. Mickey saw himself in neither extreme—and or both.

Mickey wanted God to decide. Because he couldn't say he'd done the right or the wrong moves. He'd only done what he thought he had to, one thing after the next, and now here he was at a YMCA.

Nonresident men, their hair combed and their clothes clean like business, blurred past Mickey in unscuffed running shoes and unruffled shorts, or gym bags with the shoes and or shorts inside, on their route to the courts or the sauna or the pool or the weights. They asked Mickey for change, he punched the alphabet and number keys; they paid their monthly membership installments, Mickey punched the alphabet and number keys.

"It's the Wild West, Oscar," Mickey said. "No two ways about it. You never know what might come through that door."

Mr. Crockett was over by those glass doors, his chair too close, his cane stuck out between his legs, rocking, sunning his eyes. Mickey was bent into the countertop from the inside, attentive for more business. He felt like he was getting good in this new career.

Oscar, his gray uniform shirt and pants as crisp and ironed as ever, his gray pomaded hair neatly ducktailed, didn't say much to Mickey. He thought much of what Mickey said wasn't ordinary for desk clerks. Sometimes Oscar wasn't sure if it wasn't his English or Mickey's Spanish.

"So how's maintenance, Oscar?" Mickey asked. "Maybe you don't know it, but if you want to live here, you get an employee discount. Gimme a little more time and I can probably cut you a better deal, once I catch on to the entire system."

"Te gusta?" Oscar asked suddenly, passing up Mickey's offer, pushing forward to a subject they had a mutual interest in. "You like it?"

Mickey didn't know what Oscar was talking about.

"Atrás. En la oficina."

In the office where the heavy, graying German lady, Mrs. Schweitz, did the bookkeeping, there was a younger woman behind her. This young woman was dark, a morena, with straight black hair and two glistening silver hoops swinging from her earlobes. It was hard to tell if she were good looking or not because she wore a dress that was almost the duplicate of that worn by Mrs. Schweitz, who was, to put it politely, matronly built; the dress on the young woman hung so loosely, you couldn't see her figure.

"She don't speak no Spanish," Oscar told him conspiratorially. Mickey wasn't sure what to make of Oscar's point, if that were bad or good. It did concern him that he hadn't noticed her before this. She'd been only ten feet away from where he was. "Y cómo quieres pasar el tiempo con esa?'' he asked Oscar. ''You think someday she'll help you sweep the floors?''

That made Oscar laugh a good one, though he wasn't quite sure either. ''You like the women?'' he asked in English.

Mickey might have taken offense if he didn't suspect it were only a translation problem. ''No, not both of them. Tell you what, you take the smart one, I'll take the dumb one.''

Oscar was pretty impressed by Mickey's joke.

''I know you, Oscar,'' Mickey said. ''You like the big one because . . . ,'' and he cupped his hands to his chest to indicate hefty breasts.

''Better her daughter,'' Oscar said more confidentially. ''Her daughter speaks Spanish a little.''

Mickey shook his head with fake disapproval. ''Qué pues, hombre?!''

''**M**ária,'' she said, accenting the first vowel when Mickey asked her name. Mickey wanted to find out if she had a voluptuous figure under all that fabric she wore. Legs, arms. He felt like he was in love.

''Mickey,'' he told her, holding out his hand.

Often Mickey would step backward from his desk and talk to Mária, and often Mária, whose job was to help Mrs. Schweitz with whatever she was doing—sorting through papers of some kind—would talk to him with so little friction that, on the surface, talking to Mickey might have appeared to be in her job description. More than once, Mrs. Schweitz lifted herself from her chair and politely excused herself. Either because her heart weakened amid the beauty of youthful romance, or because she really did have to go to the powder room. Or, maybe, as Mickey came to hear the rumor, to complain in the offices farther down the hall.

Mickey *had* lost some focus on desk clerking. People would pressure him, wanting things having to do with the cash register or mail or messages or information about athletic goings-on. Or the phone would ring and Mickey'd be expected to answer it. As the days on the job passed, these minor duties had become so easy for him to do they were more irritating and distracting than anything else. Better to talk with Mária, who'd stay late to tell him about what she was learning in school. She was in college, the junior college, and this was her first part-time job. Both topics of interest for Mickey, and he suggested they talk more often, but she refused to give Mickey her address or her home phone number. She wouldn't even let Mickey get near enough to touch her. Except once. Once she let Mickey kiss her when he walked her out the doors and a few steps down the block. He swore he'd follow her all the way home if she didn't let him. It was only one kiss, but her lips were as moist as olives, as tender as flower petals. That was the time Mickey, on his way out, asked Mrs. Schweitz to catch the phone for a minute, and she had generously agreed to it, and when Mickey returned to the desk he felt new purpose in his life. So he didn't like a bit the attitude of the pair of men, roof joggers, who'd been waiting for him impatiently.

"Here I am!" Mickey told the bigger one. "What the fuck you complaining about?"

"You don't have a right to cuss me!"

"Cuss you? Whadaya mean? I didn't cuss you!"

"Man, where do they find 'em," the bigger guy said to his friend.

"You can find me right here," Mickey came back. "You can find me right now."

The bigger guy was mad but didn't pursue it. Mickey punched the right keys and gave back change, victorious.

Charles Towne was waiting too. "You got some mail for me?"

As part of his job, Mickey had learned to sort the mail when the bundle was left there during his shift. Resident mail he put in the resident mailboxes, the rest went to a wire basket on Mrs. Schweitz's desk.

"Guess it already came today, Charles."

"You sure?" He scowled at Mickey, not willing to believe him.

"Like I said Charles, I think it already came today. I looked in my box too."

"I don't like nobody messing with my mail. I need my mail."

"Charles, I understand you one hundred percent."

Charles Towne, fuming, couldn't breathe for seconds. "I want my mail when it come."

Mickey couldn't think of what else to say. "You got my word on it."

Finally Mária surrendered her phone number. The office phone had a long extension cord and could reach all the way to the stool by the cash register, and the two weekdays Mária didn't come in at all—she was there for three hours Monday, Wednesday, Thursday—Mickey used this phone in the afternoon at every occasion during his hours, until Fred, as they were changing shift, mentioned how this had to stop because Fuller didn't like it. So, to be cooperative, Mickey began calling after the sun went down, after nine P.M., when the athletic area was closed. It was so much easier, Mickey wondered why he hadn't thought of it before.

Mickey felt pleased with and confident about how well it was developing between Mária and him until she started talking about her religion. The more of which he learned—that God and Jesus were very personal friends of hers, that she didn't any longer need to go to priests to discuss sins or forgiveness—the less happy he became. He tried to be patient with her. He tried to reason. He offered her the hope of love, its gentleness and purity. He explained how body and spirit sometimes united through secret paths. He told her how he too loved God and Jesus and, with his eyes shut, how he had come to love the beauty of their one short and small kiss. She liked it too, he knew it. How could she not remember that? How could she deny this? Why would Jesus or God deny her such a human pleasure, why would either of Them not want the two of *them* to explore the simple and ordinary joys offered in this short life?

And then Mária threw a story back at him. She said that, though once she saw things as he did, she had suffered for it. She had loved a bad man, and she had fallen so far down, so low, she had given herself to anything he asked of her, until she didn't know the difference between love and fear.

"I was so scared and depressed I didn't know what I could do, so I went to a simple white church to help me with this burden. It was so beautiful inside, with music and kind, caring people, even though I couldn't see that yet because I was so lost in worry. I was so tired with my heaviness. I came to pray to be free of it. I kneeled, closed my eyes. Then suddenly I was lifted out of the church building and I was on a cloud. The sun was above, and the cloud was so yielding, and I looked around and God was right over there, I recognized Him. I was so happy! I wanted to tell Him all my troubles, everything, and so I started talking and talking. He was picking all-colored flowers and putting them in a straw basket. I was trying so hard to tell Him about my sorrows, but He wouldn't say anything back. Then He held up His hand, and I understood that He didn't need to hear me. He picked more flowers and put them in the basket, and then put the basket next to me. At that moment I realized why He wasn't answering me. He gave me the basket of flowers as a gift but also to remind me that He would provide all, give me, give us, everything we need right when we need it, no sooner, no later. Exactly when we need it. I understood that nothing is unintentional, and that we are God's vessels, and I felt so much peace inside me. I had never known such peace. It became slow. I forgot time. I felt like I was God's smile. I heard sweet music, like guitars, and I was floating, like I had become the cloud. Gradually I was again inside the church and I heard the preacher talking, and I heard human voices again, I heard human music. I'd had this vision. I'd seen Him with my own eyes. Nothing is unintentional. Now *we* have met. Our meeting is not unintentional. Do you see that, do you understand that? Now I've told you.''

Even when room 412 was the darkest, light switches off, rain clouds cutting down on moon and star and streetlight, the curtain glowed yellow. There was something about that yellowness that stayed with Mickey even while his eyes were closed. Yellow was a color of meaning in the darkness. Yellow was the color of trying to fall asleep.

Mickey'd say it was the only way that he could fall asleep. He didn't like it, but it worked: Ball in a hoop or net or being caught or hit. Ball in the air, then not, then in the air, then not.

"It's hard to believe," a voice is saying, "hard to believe. People aren't *born* to talent. 'Least I like to think otherwise. Practice, that's what I want it to be about. And determination, will."

Ball drops.

"But not everybody comes up the same way," another voice says. "There's a past you don't see or know about. And then the gift just shows itself. Guys like this, well, you give them room."

"How do you see it?" one of the voices asks him.

"I play as hard as I can. Try to relax, have fun. I'm always trying to get better, working on my weaknesses. I practiced a lot in the off-season. I used to work the most on defense, but I've been spending more and more time on my offense, and it seems to be paying off."

"I guess so!"

"I'm not satisfied. I think I can get better. I'll keep doing the best I can."

Image of a ball in a hole or net or being caught or hit. Ball in the air, then not, then in the air, then not. Then not. Then not.

Mickey, already strong physically, was getting stronger by the day, but his brains weren't doing parallel workouts and were winded. Mária, he would say, did not deliver to him the personal message from God he was searching for—her tale was untrue, Mickey was certain, because her description was so corny and clichéd. A person seeing God would have drawn a more unique description, more adjectives and nouns and verbs. Besides which, he wanted *direct* confirmation, not a dopey witness. He was no simpleminded believer. Still, it did unnerve him that what she had said coincided with some of his own mumblings—look for the meaning, look for the purpose and design, keep the eyes open. And her message *was* so practical: Nothing is unintentional. Not meeting Oscar, not meeting Fred, not meeting Mr. Crockett, Ema or Lola or Mrs. Schweitz, not seeing Blind Jimmy, not hearing the man from Michigan or the Sarge jerking off or Butch, his fuzzy brown head hanging around with a beer can, sipping and whispering, not having Charles Towne wait on mail *just like he was.*

Didn't it also explain Mickey? He had to. He was *obligated* to impress these guys with exaggerations. It was intended, necessary for reasons he himself could not be conscious of. No other explanation fit so neatly.

"And you been getting the nasty from this bitch?" Omar asked. Omar Gonzalez was a new resident who met Mickey through Butch.

Mickey hadn't said anything like this yet, not to Butch, not to the Sarge. This was part of the situation: Even when he didn't say jack, something had become so expected that saying nothing was saying something.

"I never said that," Mickey replied. "I barely know her."

So Mickey didn't say yes but didn't say no. Did they think he was being modest? Because Omar and Butch appeared to be more impressed. More so Omar. Butch was always impressed—the same anyway.

"You got to help me with my woman," Omar begged Mickey. "I need a dude like yours's help bad." The thing about Omar was that, while he sounded like he meant it, he also sounded like he didn't.

Omar was not too tall and was a little overweight. He was light-skinned, with dark brown hair that coated him not only on his face as a beard, but his chest and back; because of its stiff, wire texture, it didn't cooperate well—like Omar himself. Omar was a mixed metaphor. Blue tattoos *Born to Die* and *x13x*

PoR VidA centered on his triceps were trouble and fear, but not the weirdo mix of navy blue polyester slacks, a brand-new, very white tank top shirt, and old tennis shoes. And then there was his talk. Omar enunciated, just enough, so that his voice had a childish resonance to it, which, combined with his appearance, made everything he said seem both self-conscious and unconscious, mocking and innocent.

Omar's room was on the third floor, and Mickey and Butch visited him when Mickey's shift was over. Omar was a plasterer and had found a good-paying job on a city public works project. He didn't think it was good money. Since he was from L.A., he was union, so he made half of what he felt he and any other skilled plasterer deserved. Neither Butch nor Mickey could be sympathetic, since neither had had a job close to that kind of money.

"A vato's got to have more change to get the real long-legged ones," he said. "He got to be able to buy them a bouquet of flores lindas. Then he got to take them out for a fine spread, take them for a few tragitos at a dark expensive bar, take them to a *ready* crib, play *fine* music muy linda y suave, on a *fine* stereo . . . How's he gonna get this shit when they want to pay him in pesos?"

"That's what Mária told me," Mickey put in. "She told me that God gave her these pretty flowers and then put out like a tablecloth to serve French food. No drinks, but still." He shook his head.

Omar stared a lot—something between a sneer and a smirk. "And you're getting the nasty from that bitch?" he quizzed once more.

"I didn't say I was."

"It's all right, you don't got to say nothing," said Omar. "I always hear how you dudes in Chuco are like that." His glance at Butch could have been a wink.

Butch, a cold can of beer in his hand, made what went as his laugh. Omar poured some whiskey for all of them in plastic throwaway cups, and tossed his back. Mickey followed. He and Omar, sharing a quart of beer, chased the shots with a swig from the brown bottle. Butch sipped whiskey as steadily as he did his tall boy.

Omar explained that he'd taken the bus from San Fernando to El Paso because this was where Lucy came, on a bus, when she left him. He was going to find her and then she wasn't going to get away from him again. He *would* find her, he *would* have her back, he said. He'd beg her. He'd buy her anything, take her anywhere, he would *do* anything she wanted—*anything,* he hinted at Mickey and Butch suggestively. Omar liked to share his knowledge of her ample body. "My God!" Omar pronounced, pained, then he stood up, filled his cup with another shot of whiskey, jerked it back, and rushed to the window, which he opened frantically. His room was on the street side just like Mickey and the Sarge's, and once the window was open they could hear cars alongside a cold wind that shook the yellow curtains. Omar scooted his desk chair over and stood on it, then inserted his thick upper torso into the window, gripping his hands on the aluminum sill, arching his body into the darkness, and screamed, in that peculiar singsong of his voice, as loud as he possibly could:

"Lucy! Fucking Lucy! Lucy, you bitch, you fucking whore! Lucy, where are you, where fucking are you?! Lucy, who the fuck are you *fucking* now?!"

Any day, Mickey would remind himself. Any day it'd be over, it'll be taken care of. He knew it would be very soon. *Knew* in his *bones.* It came to him by something like a message, like sixth sense. Like intuition. Which he trusted. *Knew.*

At work, when he got the chance, Mickey'd check in the

boxes, every one of them, just to make sure a letter to him didn't get put accidentally in the wrong slot. Or before his shift he might ask Fred about the mail—Mickey was sure his interest didn't seem obsessive. Leave it for me if you want, he'd propose to Fred, 'cuz I like to do it. Gives me something else to do. If you want, he'd tell Fred, pretending to be indirect, offhanded. But Fred never left the mail unsorted if it were delivered to him. Fred flipped through the envelopes methodically, indifferent. Mickey, trying not to seem too obvious, watched Fred whenever he was around. Fred would grab hold of the rubber-banded bundle of mail and turn it into two loose piles, one for residents and one for YMCA business. Fred would even stop what he was doing if someone came to the desk for some other purpose—Mickey considered taking over, but never did. Fred would leave three piles—two sorted and one unsorted—right on the formica counter, unwatched and un-protected, and walk to the back office. It was hard for Mickey to wait for Fred's return.

"So'd I get anything today?" Mickey asked Fred.

"Nothing so far." Fred had his reading glasses on his nose and didn't look up.

"Damn, Fred. I'm waiting for that check with a bunch of zeros, you know?" Mickey thought that would make his eyes twitch, but nothing unsteadied Fred. "Say, does Charles come around and ask you about the mail?"

Fred didn't respond immediately. "Who?"

"Charles. Towne."

He nodded his head slightly. "Black man, wears a baseball cap."

"That's him."

"He asks every day maybe twice, sometimes three and four times."

"Nervous about it, don't you think?"

"People living here," said Fred, adjusting his western-cut shirt as he got more comfortable on the stool, "ask all kind of questions."

"You lived here ever?"

Fred sighed, snickered, leaned back on his stool some, like it was the end of his shift. "Nope."

"Let me do that for you. Give me something to do during my shift. Help you out." Mickey couldn't let it lay.

Fred wasn't in the habit of looking people in the eye, either out of shyness or contempt, it was hard to say. But he stared at Mickey. "You can do *something* for me."

"Sure. Name it." Mickey was hopeful.

"You can't say anything about it."

Fred was never secretive or intimate and he was making Mickey very curious.

"No problem. It's between you and me."

Fred chewed on it for a second, then reached to his back pocket, unfolded his leather wallet, and pulled out a bill. "A pint of vodka."

Mickey tried not to crack one about Indians and firewater. "Not whiskey?" he did ask with a straight face, not able to resist everything.

"Vodka," Fred said again in a voice more subtle than his usual.

"**W**ho is it?!" Mickey'd been deep asleep and jumped like he'd done something wrong.

"The maid. Isabel."

Mickey blinked his eyes around the dark, yellowed room. He couldn't name what there was to worry about or why he did. It had taken him forever to get any sleep. Hours of imagined interviews and interrogations about the good and the bad, hours of sporting events and interviews with the stars. He'd gotten up and done push-ups and sit-ups. Nothing had worked except that clearly he'd fallen asleep because someone'd told him he had to wake up.

"I have to change the sheets," Isabel said from the other side of the door.

Mickey didn't want her to come in. He didn't feel like having company. Nevertheless, he stood up and unlocked and opened the door.

Isabel hesitated because Mickey was standing in his jeans and nothing else, his hair tangled and his eyes glazed. It was one o'clock in the afternoon.

Mickey sat there while she changed the sheets. He thought of saying something to her. Something nice. Something to make conversation. He visualized lying in bed with her, how she'd be without clothes, whether her extra weight would make her more or less desirable to him. He imagined a conversation about asking her out. Asking her if she were married. Joking with her to say yes even if she were married. He could talk to people. He could talk to women. To this Isabel. Like when he went up to Ema. Remember? He kissed her, she let him. She wanted to go out with him. Her mother wouldn't let her. Why shouldn't Isabel like him too? And Mária. *That* was for real. That really happened.

Without saying a word, Isabel exchanged the dirty and wrinkled linen for the clean and pressed, tucking the top sheet and blanket snug and neat under the mattress, fluffing out the small pillow, letting it rest perfectly centered at the head of the bed. Not moving from his desk chair, Mickey didn't utter a word until she was about to leave. Thanks, he said. She closed the door behind her, then glanced back at Mickey just as she might at any man in the hall.

"**W**hy do you *think* he cut my hours?" Mickey asked Mrs. Schweitz. The latest scheduling had Fred and a weekend desk clerk putting in an extra day each, which reduced Mickey to three days a week instead of five.

Mickey still believed that Mrs. Schweitz was much more warm-blooded than the blue-eyed gaze she iced her paperwork with, that mush was underneath the husky physique taming her office chair. So far, she wasn't hot or soft on this discussion Mickey led, simply incapable of shutting him off.

"I don't know, honestly, I don't know," she told him.

"You think I should go have a talk with him?"

"If you want." She turned her face, guilty, toward the work on her desk, trying to not make her lack of interest obvious.

Mickey didn't receive her signals. "Seems like he could give me an explanation. Don't you think so?"

"I don't know." She shuffled through some papers.

"You think it has anything to do with me and Mária?"

"I'm not sure." She readjusted her bulk to the office chair, stretched the muscles in her neck.

"So why did he let Mária go?"

Mrs. Schweitz shook her head in his direction, her pain as undisguised as she could make it without groaning.

"Pinche hijo de la chingada," Mickey sniped.

Mrs. Schweitz beamed her nose back to paperwork again, praying she'd heard the end of it.

"Didn't that jerk explain anything to her either?"

"Not much," she said, reversing field, defensive now. It was her boss he was calling names.

Mickey hadn't heard any subtlety in her answer, caught no intonation. "It ain't fair. It ain't right."

He left the office area because of Fred, who was standing over by the cash register.

"He didn't give you an explanation either?" Mickey asked him.

Fred barely seemed to recognize Mickey. He slid his glasses out from the case clipped to his shirt pocket, then ran his fingers down the scheduling sheet, stubbing the new blocks of time he was supposed to be at the desk. "Has me for eight hours of overtime." He shook his head again, grimacing, lifting the glasses off his ears and nose. "Whadaya gonna do," he said, resigned.

"You didn't want extra hours, did you?"

"I sure did not."

"I can't understand it."

Fred said nothing.

"What do *you* think?"

"About what?" Fred asked.

Playing handball with the Sarge had turned so critical and serious that Mickey was almost losing much of the pleasure in it, but he still kept on winning anyway. He couldn't do otherwise. It was as though it were out of his hands, willed from a source not his. He did feel sorry for the Sarge. The Sarge wanted it so bad, the Sarge needed the gratification of winning. But Mickey didn't know how to lose, Mickey was unable to lose.

Though one game it got close. It was the last in a set and Mickey was up 17–15 and the Sarge took back the serve. He won two points quickly with perfect kill shots. Then he served a high lob to Mickey's left hand, close to the wall, at the corner. Mickey stumbled over his feet just enough as he swung, hitting his hand against the white wall while the hard black ball smacked right below his wrist. He cried out.

"It's like I broke my hand, Elias!" he yelped, squirming around the court. "It fucking hurts!"

The Sarge, hot and sweating, had been playing all out like it was war. Angry, his red blood pumped purple into his dark skin. "So you want to *quit?*"

"I don't know if I can keep playing," Mickey told him.

The Sarge paced. "That's just like you," he said. "That's just the kind of *man* you are!"

"What are you trying to say?"

"You know exactly!"

"No, I don't think I do!"

"You want to *quit* right now, right when you think you're going to *lose!*"

"You gotta be kidding. You aren't kidding?"

The Sarge spun away, more than pissed off. "Guys like you," he steamed.

Mickey laughed at him. "Pues, you got it then, boss! Gimme a second, nada más." He shook and rubbed his hand. What always hurt most in handball was the ball smacking the wrist—close to being slugged in the balls, it sapped energy. His fingers weren't swollen more than in any normal game, that didn't bother him.

So they played it out and Mickey won 21–19. He almost felt bad about it. He kind of wished he'd lost. Once he got the serve, though, it was out of his control. Then again, the Sarge was an asshole—he wished Big Ears played handball—and he deserved it.

As upset as he was, the Sarge still insisted on the coffee shop after the game. It was the routine, and Sarge gripped hard on the routine.

Lola poured them both very hot coffee. "There you are my hone-neys."

Mickey laid back for a few too-silent minutes. "What we need, no offense meant, is Consuela," said Mickey, "not Lola."

The Sarge scowled at him, then tried to sip his coffee, even past his tightened lips.

"You know who Consuela is? Don't get confused that she don't go by the name Consuelo like she would in Mexico. It's how they spell it in the Wild West."

The Sarge couldn't respond if he tried.

"Consuela is the one that Big Jake saves from the Apaches," Mickey explained.

Directly across from the horseshoe counter where Mickey and the Sarge were sitting was the man from Michigan, who pretended to be reading the paper but was really listening.

"See, Big Jake runs off the Apaches' horses over by the Hueco Mountains, at the tanks, and sneaks in and cuts the throat of the indio left behind to guard over her. Big Jake is part-Indian too, I think that's right, so he's good at this stuff."

Almost like a massage, the muscles in the Sarge's jaw loosened, which seemed to also let the rest of his body sink, relaxed, into the mushroom stool.

"You should see this Consuela! Even after she got beat up by those Indians she's a killer—skin as smooth and rich as gold, eyes like dark chocolate."

"What *are* you talking about?" the Sarge asked, something like a smile breaking through.

"Consuela. She got captured then raped by renegade indios, so Jake saves her and starts riding away. And he . . . well, he *tends* to her up in an abandoned mining shack on the Franklin Mountains, where all these prairie dog and snake holes are, and at night he starts warm fires of dried cholla and mesquite, and he eats jackrabbit and rattlesnake meat, and he listens to coyotes howl at the moon."

Both the Sarge and the man from Michigan used their ears like eyes on Mickey, who was telling this story with an off-the-mark sincerity.

"Now Jake, who you know is no angel himself, he loves Consuela like any of us would, both in the gentleman's way and that other way. But he also has promised to bring her back to the hacienda where she belongs, back to the Don, her father, an old buddy of Jake's, who the Don still insists on calling Jacobo, being he's like an honorary mejicano, he's done such badass shit."

Mickey drank some of his coffee, and almost before he put it down Lola was filling it up again.

"I *reckon* Jake's got some *mighty* big trouble," Mickey told the Sarge. "It's like I been telling ya. You gotta keep on your toes. Gotta stay alert and protect the beautiful women. Gotta keep the old Colt oiled and loaded. You never know what danger the stranger might bring."

The middle-aged man in the gray suit and tie—the clothes were off, weren't right, like a city boy dressing cowboy—reminded Mickey of the man who came for Blind Jimmy that day. It might have been him, Mickey couldn't be sure. The younger man he walked in with smiled with gigantic incisors, and his eyeballs seemed to have been preserved in a thick oil, they were so swollen and greasy and foreign to the man's sockets. He wore old jeans, though not worn at the knees, and a polo shirt a size too large, and he carried a hard, square suitcase.

"This is the Reverend Miller Johnson Holcombe the Third," the man in the suit said of the other.

Mickey wasn't sure how he was supposed to respond to such royalty, or why he was even being introduced, so he didn't say anything until it struck him that nothing more would be said until he did. "So is there something I can do for you two?"

"We need a room," the man in the suit said.

"Can't have rooms together," Mickey told him, taking a pose on the stool. "Only one person to a room."

"No no, I didn't mean that." He laughed for emphasis. "The reverend needs the room, not me."

"Okay," said Mickey. The man in the suit expected another sentence from Mickey, but Mickey decided not to be easy this time.

The Reverend Miller stood upright behind the impending transaction, proud of himself and his stature, important. "Could he get a room?" the man finally asked on his behalf.

"Sure he could."

The man was mystified by Mickey's procedure. Mickey was enjoying being difficult.

"You have available rooms?" the man continued.

"With or without a bathroom?" Mickey said.

"Well," the man said, shifting his concentration, looking to the reverend for the rest now. The reverend wasn't helping him. He was beaming grandly, preoccupied with a larger issue only he was aware of. "What's the difference?" the man in the suit asked.

"Shitting or showering in the room by yourself, or shitting or showering down the hall with everybody else." Mickey was very pleased with himself for taking the opportunity to say this.

"The rate," the man said. "I mean difference in the nightly cost."

"Four or five-fifty a day, twenty-four or thirty-three a week."

The man in the suit added and subtracted as he stared away from the reverend. Then he took out a wallet from his back pocket and handed Mickey eight dollars. "Well," he told the reverend, "I do wish you lots of luck." He held out a limp hand, relieved, for the reverend, who grasped and shook it meaningfully.

"May God bless," spoke the Reverend Miller, implying that he influenced such matters.

Both Mickey and the reverend waited until the man in the gray suit had made it out the glass doors to attend to one another.

"If you decide to stay for a week, you have to pay it all by the fourth day and then you'll get the seventh day free," Mickey told the reverend, sliding a registration card across the formica counter. He punched the numbers and the letters on the register and deposited the cash.

The reverend pushed the card back to Mickey. The only thing he filled out was the name, Reverend Miller J. Holcombe III, and city, where first he wrote, then crossed out, El Paso. He leaned in at Mickey, too close, too familiar, and said, "I'm able to receive mail here, correct? I'm expecting extremely important mail." He winked and smiled like he and Mickey had an understanding. "It's very, very important."

"The room key here," Mickey said, holding it up, "opens a mailbox right over there."

The reverend winked again, then looked around, muddled.

"The elevator's behind you," Mickey pointed out.

The reverend showed Mickey his rotting teeth thankfully, and, with sensitivity, without aggression, tapped the UP button.

When Mickey heard the Sarge's bed slapping against the other side of his wall this particular night he couldn't stand it, so he shoved open his door just in time to catch the man across cutting yet another loose. Mickey stomped down the hall in his dirty socks—he had washed them once since he'd been here—and kicked open the restroom door hard. This time another fourth-floor resident, a Mr. Smith, was at the sink running water, entranced with himself in the mirror, not the slightest disturbed or disrupted by Mickey's noisy entrance. Mr. Smith was a longtime resident and well known at the Y because he gave money to the poor neighborhood children who hung out at the basketball courts, which generated unconfirmed gossip about his real interests. Mickey didn't believe any of it for a simple reason—the man was so ugly and gross that no kids would be alone with him for any amount of money.

Mickey had paused to calm himself. It was late at night, or early in the morning—two in the morning. Mr. Smith turned his head toward Mickey and smiled a phony smile, polite in a symbolic way. Then, moving his head again, said hello into the mirror. Mickey said hello back to the Mr. Smith in the mirror.

Mickey visited the urinal with his eyes on the man just in case. But Mr. Smith continued, ritually, to splash the water on his face several more times, then admired the image in the mirror, then splashed more water. He was smiling continuously.

Mickey left Mr. Smith, walked back to his room, and shut the door gently, resigned. It was quiet now but Mickey was still disturbed. Mickey would say this was when he went back down the hall and made a collect telephone call. He'd say this and that he'd called two other times already and there never was an answer. This time, he'd say, an operator told him that service had been disconnected. He asked her if she'd gotten it right and he repeated the phone number, and she said she had but she tried again for him anyway—she still got the disconnect recording.

Afterward, the door closed—he was worried and afraid— Mickey said his mind ran through it until it ran into something else hovering inside there, then over him, around him, beneath and through him. He felt serious ideas cross his mind: No letter, no mail. No letter, no money. No money . . . The vision came on dark, darker than the room. The vision came on as ugly as death. The vision made Mickey more afraid. Mickey tried to shape it, draw a picture, color in the spaces. But all he could see was Mr. Smith. That had to be because that's who he'd just seen in the bathroom. He looked like the Sarge. Mickey started doing push-ups and he did a hundred and seventy-five of them. Then he did a hundred more. Then a hundred and fifty more. His arms finally sore, he did sit-ups, and while he did pleasant ideas formed: It was going to end soon, something was going to happen, and he wouldn't be in this room 412 at the YMCA much longer.

"What about this criticism of you, that you're not really a team player?"

"I'm not sure what you mean."

"Sure you do. You know. You're not loyal to the other players on your team. You keep to yourself too much."

"I don't think that's true. We get along."

"That's enough? To get along?"

"Look, one of the problems I have is getting these kind of questions thrown at me just because I'm playing better than other guys. How can I say anything? What am I supposed to say?"

"But can one player be *too* good? Can't that hurt the team's morale?"

"Maybe if he thinks he's superior to the others."

"You don't think that about yourself?"

"Of course not."

"You are better, though."

"I'm playing better. I do the best I can. I keep to myself, that's all. There's nothing wrong with that, is there?"

Guy goes off, practicing before the game. Everybody else likes him, but those others have to look for something, have to dig at him. They're not like fans. He practices, shoots. He knows it's the game. As long as he wins, he wins. If he loses, he loses. He doesn't play to win or lose, only to play. He can't lose if he isn't trying to win. That's his strength. That's his strength. He shoots the ball. The ball. The ball.

M ickey was on duty and no business was happening and so he called Mária from the desk. Most of the young residents were playing ping-pong, while the older ones were in the TV room, the volume up too high. Mickey hadn't talked to Mária much since her speech, whose significance, for him, was only to discourage a more intimate relationship. Now what he wanted was to learn the details of why she'd lost her job.

"How you been?"

"I'm okay," she said casually. Then she corrected herself. "I've been just fine." Said more affirmative, more upbeat.

"They cut me back too," Mickey said. "My hours. They cut me out of two days."

"Really?"

Mickey wasn't sure how to talk to her. He hadn't approached figuring her out. He assumed she'd be angry about losing the job, would want to complain and even hear out his complaints, and then compare, they could compare. He assumed she'd be at least normal about this subject.

"Yeah," he continued. "They didn't even tell me why. Mr. Ears didn't even give me an explanation." He waited for her to add something but nothing returned. "What about you?"

"If it's God's will," she told him after a pause. "There's no reason to get upset."

Mickey wanted to groan. Then he realized that maybe he did catch something of *her* feelings.

"Upset about what?" he asked.

"I don't care what they say," Mária said.

"About what?" Mickey was thinking it'd be gossip about him and her, along the lines of what the guys, especially Omar, teased him about. "I didn't touch the mail, never," she said.

Mickey lost his breath. He couldn't talk.

"I thought Mrs. Schweitz would know that. I'm a Christian, you know, and I wouldn't steal now."

Mickey still couldn't think fast enough to reply to her.

"God knows me," she went on, "and I don't have to account to anyone else. Only Him, and Him alone."

"Yeah," Mickey got out. "Yeah."

"We have to trust God's will and purpose," she said. "You understand what I mean, don't you?"

"Sure," Mickey said. He had to seem enthusiastic to encourage her, to not break the conversation off. "Yeah," he got out, "I been hearing about missing mail."

"Nothing is unintentional," she reminded him.

He couldn't make that connection in any fashion. "So you didn't take it, is that it?"

He felt weak. God and the mail. What could this mean? The air was too light, and Mickey had an overwhelming sense that something was going to happen, and he didn't have a notion of what he should do about it. This sound of hers, this conversation, was, somehow, evidence: not its truth or untruth, just the linkage of subjects, the tone, the exchange of words, all of it blended into a chant, a musical backdrop.

Right then Omar and Butch rounded the corner from the ping-pong room.

"Aren't you going to let that dude in?" Omar asked.

Mickey hadn't heard the man outside in the dark pounding on the glass door.

"Look Mária, I gotta go," he told her, hanging up before he heard what she said, before he knew what he himself was doing.

"Mária, eh?" Omar teased. "You still doing nasty with that bitch?"

Mickey unlocked the doors. The man who came in wore a denim jacket and matching pants. He stomped his boots into the linoleum tile like it'd been snowing and he'd been covered with it. "Goddamn cold!" he shouted, rubbing his hands together. "And you blabbing on the goddamn phone!" But once he elbowed up to the front desk, and Mickey squeaked past his swing door to the other side, the man brought his face up from under the collar he had raised to his ears and stopped himself from continuing this complaint about not being let in right away. "Hey, I know you!" he told Mickey with a warmed-up expression. "I know you!"

Omar and Butch waited. So did Mickey, who did not recognize this man standing in front of him.

"You don't remember?!"

Mickey tried to see something in the man's face. He saw wrinkled, weathered skin, he smelled alcohol all over it, whiskey, half-pints like the one bagged in the side pocket of his jacket.

"You really don't remember?" he asked Mickey.

Mickey shook his head and shrugged his shoulders.

"I was there when the police kicked you outta the Denny's restaurant!"

Mickey had almost erased the incident from his mind.

The man faced Omar and Butch, proud to relive the memory. "I was eating at the counter when he comes in. The cook owed him some money so the boy here tells him to come bring it. Now the manager's right there too and this boy has to tell how that cook owes him money and that he come to collect. Well, the manager, he's a pretty big-sized colored boy, and he don't want this Mexican boy making such a fuss in his restaurant. But the boy won't let up. Instead he starts talking at the cook directly, saying, I want twenty dollars, and I want it now. Like that, *I want it,* he says. The big colored guy, he pushes this boy here toward the door but gets himself pushed right back and told he better lay off. Now the whole restaurant is hushed up. Waitresses, busboys, those people in the booths are watching with their mouths open. He yells again, gimme my twenty dollars. He's just standing there, not moving, just expecting the money. The manager is trying to settle with him by now, talking different because now probably he's scared of this crazy Mexican and because he's stalling, since he told a waitress to get hold of the police, but the boy, he's not looking at nobody but that cook. There's two cooks and one of them quit what he's doing and is standing away from the other, who's standing over something what's sizzling and frying, and you can see how he's the one who's scared and pissing his pants, who's wishing he could stick his whole head in that white hat on his head. He's no match for the boy here, and he says, he says he don't have it, he won't have any money till pay day. This boy here don't believe it though and he yells to give him his twenty dollars and he don't move and won't. He's trying to act polite. He's real still except his voice so that everybody knows he's dangerous, somebody's maybe gonna be hurt real bad. Right then the cops get there. They each take him by an arm. He ain't fighting back, but he ain't exactly cooperating either. They talk outside, then they get in the car and they drive away."

The men waited for Mickey to finish it out, to expand with narrative, but instead Mickey dropped his head, embarrassed by it.

"You were hungry," Omar suggested. "You shoulda taken it out in eats."

"It was the principle," Mickey said, and the three men laughed like he'd cracked a joke. Mickey joined them when he realized they might be right.

The man filled out a card for a room. Mickey punched the letter and the number keys on the register, made some change, gave him a receipt and a room key, and sat back on the stool.

Mickey'd been working out with the free weights and the inclined board in the narrow, low-rent room he'd gotten used to when Charles Towne, as he did many times, stopped for a fidgety, restless glare at him. Charles probably did not mean to glare but he did, his eyes squirming with a unique kind of suspicion. Suddenly Charles barked a question at Mickey—that too wasn't unlike Charles. Usually it was about how many of what Mickey was doing had he done. Charles was in his street clothes, and Mickey thought that must mean something, so he finished some bench presses, resting the barbell above his head on the iron rack, and sat up. Charles spoke again. Since Mickey'd gotten out of the swimming pool previous to this, he pointed and said, "Water in my ears, Charles," though the reason he couldn't hear was more that Charles was mumbling as he often did.

"Better machine upstairs," Charles said. He waved Mickey forward.

Charles Towne led Mickey to the Universal weight machines reserved for the better-off members who also paid for private lockers and enjoyed the other carpeted, not linoleum, pleasures of a health club. For the next few weeks, every day, Charles stuck around to watch Mickey go from side to side on the machine, never moving himself out from under the doorway. Mickey didn't know which was worse, sneaking the use of this machine not intended for residents, or seeing, every time he looked up, Charles standing there with that tilt to his head, the slant to his eye, there like he needed to supervise. But Mickey got used to it. He got used to Charles too, and even began to enjoy him.

Charles wore a plaid shirt and baggy pants held up by suspenders, and a logoless, too-small baseball cap, which he fit crooked on his head, a little askance like he kept his eyes. But since Charles himself was a little off, he didn't deal with most people too well, and other people didn't deal with him too well either. Charles didn't mean it, Mickey would say in his defense, didn't decide to be how he was. Mickey had gotten to know Charles at the weight machine by muscling conversations that wouldn't advance any other way, and this was how he learned that Charles had grown up in New Orleans, had lived with lots of relatives and in foster homes after his mother had passed—he was very young— and had only recently arrived in El Paso. The Baptist Church was helping him out. The Baptist Church made sure he ate once a day, and he'd help them back with things as repayment. Charles Towne, who looked old, was still young.

"But why here in El Paso, Charles?"

"Because this is where I was supposed to come," he told Mickey.

"The military or something? Fort Bliss?" Mickey was seated, pushing the machine's leg weights.

"No sir."

"Jesus Christ, Charles, you don't gotta call me sir. You know?"

It seemed like Charles was going to say yes sir but got tongue-tied.

"So what is it you're doing here?" Mickey went on, not really listening carefully, since he was also trying to keep count. "You're not planning to stay here forever."

"I'm getting a job."

"Oh yeah?"

"Yes sir."

Mickey ignored it. He was still counting. "That's great, Charles." When he finished his set, he turned to Charles again, to keep up conversation. "What is it you're gonna do?"

For the first time Charles shifted the weight on his legs. Charles, like Fred, could never hold his eyes steady onto another person's eyes for very long, but this time he wouldn't even allow himself to focus on Mickey's chin.

Mickey smelled blood. What he really wanted to know about was Charles's obsession with the mail.

"Come on, Charles. What's the plan?"

"Be working for the government," Charles said reluctantly. He was shy and hesitant, anxious.

"That ain't much to go on," Mickey urged him, friendly. "What is it, secret work?"

"Yes sir." Charles went into a whisper.

Mickey laughed, then cut it short. He was kidding, but Charles was not kidding. "Secret work, huh, Charles?"

"Yes . . ." He forced himself not to say sir.

Mickey's legs pumped the weights again. "What kind of secret work, Charles? A secret agent or something?"

Charles nearly lost his balance. "Yes sir, that's right, exactly." Charles was agitated. "How'd you know?"

Mickey kept driving the leg weights, pushing his laughter out through his toes. "A secret agent." He didn't think anybody'd ever believe him if he repeated this.

Charles couldn't move, the shock freezing him under the doorway. Mickey finished the set, then shifted over to the machine's bench press. He was setting the key when Mr. Fuller, in an unbuttoned blue suit, a matching blue tie lying against the white shirt, pushed his way past Charles.

"What are *you two* doing here? You two do not belong in here and you'll have to leave." Mr. Fuller was angry, though he was the kind that didn't flaunt it, who feared showing too much hostility even when that was the honest emotion. He phonied a politeness. "Right now." Then, as afterthought, "Please."

"Ain't nobody else here in the morning!" Charles spoke up, mad. "Not *ever!*"

"That doesn't matter. You'll still have to leave."

"We ain't doing nothing bad," Charles told him. "Ain't nobody using it."

"You'll still have to leave. Now." Fuller was speaking directly to Mickey, and, no more needing to be said, he disappeared down the hall as silently as he'd come.

Caught and guilty, Mickey jumped off the foam-padded red bench like he'd been caught with a cigarette in high school. He shrugged at Charles with embarrassment.

"You weren't doing nothing bad," Charles said, defending him. "That's bullshit."

"Thanks, Charles, but it's okay."

"That's bullshit. That man just doing mean and don't like us. He don't understand. He doing mean."

Mickey listened.

* * *

It was a windy night, and cold, yet Omar left his window open, and the yellow curtains flapped. He'd come in late but also with a six-pack, which he was sharing with Butch and Mickey. Omar said he was depressed. There was no telling with Butch how he was feeling. In any case it was, except for the wind, too quiet. The three men sat there with light jackets on, none of them even considering sliding the window shut.

So Mickey found himself talking, trusting them more than he trusted anyone. Mickey wouldn't tell them all of the circumstances, he wouldn't, but he told them about being on the West Coast, and he said how he'd been into this thing there but he didn't want to say what it was exactly, they just had to take his word on it because that was best for them all. He told them how he came back here, ended up at the Y, how he was waiting. Told them how, at the beginning, he'd been confident that the deal was going to work out, but that now, after all this time, he wasn't sure. How now he was afraid something real bad might happen, but he wouldn't guess what. Not exactly anyway. Just how it would be bad. Something *serious*. He could be the problem now, he said. Told them how the shit might hit soon and only then was it going to be over. About how he knew, he said, like a premonition, but a strong one based on experience and information. So either good news or bad, but news, something, and soon. It *was* going to happen. Payment, or payback, he told them, if they knew what he meant. Told them he had to hole up here and make sure. How he was playing it out all the way to the end, win or lose. That that was how he thought anyway. How he wasn't sure, but how he didn't want to fuck it up, he'd been hanging in here this long.

"So whadaya think?" he asked at the end. It was like he was shuffling his feet, toeing the floor nervously, except he was sitting on a chair.

Omar seemed more disturbed about his own trouble. There was never any telling with Butch.

"How would you handle it?" Mickey asked again, now pleading for a reaction.

"Sounds tough," Omar finally commented. "Sounds like a real outlaw situation."

Mickey wanted understanding.

Butch sipped on the beer.

Oscar was leaning his gray, starched and ironed uniform into the formica counter of the front desk. Mickey bent into it from the other direction to get more personal with him.

"So that's her, huh, Oscar?"

"Yes. Just like I say too." Oscar raised his eyebrows and winked like the cad in the bad movie. He was referring to the size of her breasts. "And she speaks some Spanish too."

Mrs. Schweitz's daughter, Rosemary, had replaced Mária. Rosemary was a giant woman, maybe five-eleven, almost as tall as Mickey. And though not fat, she was far from thin. From a distance she seemed more cultured than sexy, the two confused as a result of the dress and style inappropriate for, at least not ever seen at, the Y—a sheer, flowery material and wild, wispy, long blond hair with dark roots, which parted on the side, came around and tickled her face.

"So whadaya think?" Mickey asked Oscar. "Va a ser tu amor por vida? Your *true* love? You made a mistake on that last one, you know."

"Quién sabe?" Oscar said with an old-fashioned sadness. "Quién sabe?" Oscar ran his fingers through his immaculately combed and ducktailed, elegantly grayed hair. Obviously there was a time when Oscar, a handsome man even in his fifties, was even a more handsome young man.

Oscar straightened up, and then arched his back, and then slapped the formica counter.

Mickey jumped at the opportunity. "Back to it!" Mickey loved getting to say this.

Oscar took off.

Mickey was angled on the front desk stool so that Rosemary was in his peripheral vision, and he was beginning to fall in love with her when John Hooper fisted the table on about the same spot Oscar usually slapped it.

"How's it going?" Mickey said.

"Going this way and that," John Hooper said, knuckling his cowboy hat up his forehead a little. "Still here." He handed Mickey a dollar bill he wanted changed for the soda machine. "How's the nut business?"

Mickey, distracted, wasted another second figuring out what was meant by that. "Oh yeah," he said when he caught on. "Yeah, well, you know. Whadaya gonna do? It beats the streets, it beats the Grand."

"That's why I'm here," John Hooper said, grimacing. "I just stay away from them as much as I can. I won't be here forever."

Mickey liked this guy for his hard substance, for his sharpness of opinion. "It's what I keep telling myself too," he said in an almost confessional voice. "It'd get to me if I didn't think I was gonna leave soon."

John Hooper nodded knowingly. "Take her easy, partner," he said. He left, his boots giving a pounding to the linoleum.

Mickey got back almost immediately to following the outlines under Rosemary's almost translucent fabric.

* * *

"Rosemary Schweitz," she said when Mickey asked her name. Mickey was now positive she had a luscious body, and her bad-girl eyes, though hidden and shaded by that hair in her face, commanded hope that if she had religion, it did not include abstinence or torture.

"Mickey," he replied, holding out his hand, squeezing hers just a tiny bit more than necessary.

The Sarge, his right arm lounged across the front seat of his Mercury as he turned the wheel with the left index finger on his left hand, rested the car between the white lines in the McDonald's parking lot. It was three in the afternoon, and the lot was almost empty. The muzak-free weather outside the car was as pleasant as it was behind the airtight doors, just as it was in the Muzak-regulated climate of Mac's. The Sarge and Mickey ordered their usuals.

"Beautiful day," Mickey commented once they'd sat down in a booth with a window looking onto the Franklins. "Blue sky, warm sun. Brown mountain." Mickey kept his mirror shades on. "So what is it with you and Mr. Ears?"

The Sarge frowned, ever disapproving.

"You got something on him or something?" Mickey went on.

"What's that mean?"

"I never asked you how come I got the job so easy."

"Fuller needed somebody at the desk."

"Yeah but how come he just *gave* it to me? How come he didn't ask no questions?"

The Sarge was reluctant. He bit off some of his burger and chewed.

"So where d'you know him from?"

The Sarge swallowed, then sipped some of his soda. "The army."

"Andale pues."

The Sarge went on munching.

"Compadres, buddies, huh?" It occurred to Mickey that the Sarge was being *too* mysterious. "Close friends, like that. Right?"

"That's right," the Sarge said. "Mostly."

Mickey began eating one of his fish burgers and let it drop. The Sarge, he perceived easily enough, was not welcoming this discussion. "So how come he cut my hours? You know why?"

The Sarge shook his head. "Maybe he thinks you're goofing off."

"He told you that?"

"No. It was a thought is all."

Mickey couldn't be sure whether this was the Sarge's own opinion of him or the insider view that he and Mr. Fuller and who knows else held about him. "Nobody's told me I was goofing. And I haven't heard no fucking complaints."

The Sarge looked up at Mickey over his eyebrows, in disapproval and disbelief. "Then it's probably not that. Could be that he had to lower your hours for good reasons, nothing personal."

"I don't think so," Mickey said, surly. "Besides, he should've been man enough to give me a reason to my face. You go tell him that too."

The Sarge shook his head, exhausted but forbearing. "Get another job. You should be looking around for a real job anyway. That one isn't going to last forever, and you ought to know that."

He gouged more of his burger. "Besides, I thought you didn't care about this job."

"Well, I don't," Mickey snapped. It occurred to him that they really didn't like each other too much. So why did the Sarge continue to take him places, and in general hang out with him? Maybe it wasn't only because they were partners in handball, or because of the loneliness of living at the Y. Maybe Mickey'd been too quick, too easy, to discard his early theories about the Sarge's interest in him.

"The soft and marshmallow. The calm and geezy . . ." Mickey was with Butch, sitting on the brick planter outside the glass front doors of the Y before his desk shift started. It was a warm afternoon. Cars drove by like they weren't going anywhere, like they were Mickey and Butch's entertainment. Mickey'd bought himself a quart of beer when he'd gone over to get vodka for Fred. He drank it from a free soda cup and hid the bottle behind him, under the thick, fat leaf of a century plant whose blooming stalk shot up ten feet. Butch sipped a cold tall boy from an undisguised brown bag. The subject, Mickey's, was the Sarge's music. Mickey was figuring out deejay descriptions for the muzak station. ". . . Lukewarm and lithiumed. Mashed potatoed and Ex-Laxed. Thorazined and thermaled. Valiumed and . . . hijolá, that's a hard one!"

Butch so seldom spoke that when he did, Mickey usually had to ask him again. "Makes me sleepy," Butch said louder, though still not loud.

Mickey wasn't sure if he was talking about beer or the Muzak or the Muzak list, but he'd decided to go on with that anyway when he heard something else in the distance. "Listen," he told Butch.

Butch had his eyes shut, but then opened them about as wide as they got, which was not wide, and nodded. It was an approaching ice-cream truck with a bell song: "Oh give me a home, where the buffalo roam, where the deer and the antelope play. Where seldom is heard, a discouraging word, and the sky is not cloudy all day."

"That's great, ain't it?" Mickey said fondly. Really he meant it. It really made him feel good to hear this music, sitting outside the YMCA doors with beer in him. "I'm not saying it's the greatest song in the entire hemisphere, but ain't it great for an ice-cream truck?"

Butch shrugged his shoulders, opinionless.

"I like the paloma blanca one you hear once in a while now too," Mickey said.

"You must be the expert," Butch said, loud enough.

Sarcasm? Irony? Butch usually didn't say shit, and it threw Mickey off for a minute. "I admit it ain't Chuck Berry, or Sam the Sham and the Pharaohs. Or Vicente Fernandez. Or why not the Stones? Or Chris Montes, or James Brown, or Sir Doug, or the Platters, or Marvin Gaye, or the Four Tops . . ." Mickey could have gone on but he stopped himself, since Butch didn't seem to respond well enough to another churning of a list. "But that song that's playing, that's almost the perfect one for an ice-cream truck here." He filled up the soda cup with the rest of the quart. "Don't you think so?"

Butch said something.

"Can't hear you, man," Mickey said.

". . . don't believe you," Butch said.

"You don't believe me about what?"

"Omar don't."

Mickey was willing to give it up. "You got to speak up, compita."

Butch was willing to give it up too.

The ice-cream truck music was nearer and louder. "You really don't like that shit?" Mickey asked. " 'Cuz, man, I think it's *bad*. I mean here we are, out in the Wild West, under the big blue desert sky—so there's just a little gray pollution here and there, what's new?—and where en otros tiempos vaqueros and bandidos and cherifes didn't drive four-wheel trucks with horsey names. You know? You know what I mean, qué no?"

Later at the desk Mickey remembered the broken conversation and worked it out like a puzzle.

"Omar don't believe me. Is that it?"

Butch nodded.

"Omar don't believe me about what?"

"He don't believe none of it. Don't believe none of what you say, bro."

"Ping-pong, handball, swimming?" He stopped for a second. "Which? The girls?" He stopped again. "Mária? The stuff about Califas?"

"He don't believe you, me dijo. I'm just telling you."

Mickey felt winded. "And you know I appreciate it," he told Butch.

IV

Omar bought a '63 Chevy Nova, with once upon a time bright, shiny red paint, a once upon a time pale blue interior. With a little muffler work, the V-6 engine might have sounded as strong as it seemed to run. The car had belonged to a house painter Omar worked with, and he got it cheap.

"But why not the one with the spoke wheels you bragged about?" Mickey, sitting shotgun, asked him. Omar had been talking big time about a newer Olds Toronado he'd seen, told them he'd get that to impress Lucy and her family. Butch was in the backseat with a six-pack of cold tallboys, one of which he'd snapped off the plastic vine and pointed at Omar, who took it, popping the tab between his legs. "I was expecting to ride in class," Mickey went on.

"I don't got the feria for that this week," Omar told him. As ever, there was no way to tell if even Omar believed what Omar said or not. "Besides, my baby don't love my wheels, she loves my stroke."

"Eso! You hear that, Butch?" Mickey accepted his can of beer from Butch too.

"You wait and see." Omar tilted the can, downing most of the can of beer like he was truly thirsty. He belched.

"Some impression you're gonna make on this love baby of yours," Mickey said. "Backfires and burps."

"She loves *me,*" Omar said, after he'd swallowed it all. He dropped the empty onto the floorboard and pointed at his crotch. "And she loves *this.*"

"That's what you keep telling us," Mickey said, "and I tell you, I can't wait to meet her."

The Lower Valley road they traveled was paved two-lane but Mickey didn't see it that way because of the dust rising up from it, the tumbleweeds reeling across like drugged roadrunners: In the West is where they were. Where Billy the Kid was supposed to be locked up, where John Wesley Hardin twirled a pistola and dealt cards, where Pancho Villa lived forever and Pershing became a street downtown. And out here at dusk this day, the *whoosh* from a storm chasing after the setting sun, snapping branches and shadows off the cottonwoods and electrical poles, they drove by the Mexico-style adobes from then that were still now—or if not, which sure looked like they were—called auto parts and liquor stores, fereterias and supermercados. The land was still a flat, romantic brown, the light-skinned desert sand swirling around a single ocotillo or cholla or yucca on one side of the street, the darker plowed loam on the other, in the reach of the once-wider, fertile Rio Grande, planted with cotton or alfalfa or chile.

They stopped at a house made of stone and wood roofed with bright blue asphalt tiles, a cinder-block addition the same size as the rest of the house it attached to, with a homey concrete front porch painted red, and a truck and a car—a wheelless Cadillac—on the dirt front yard.

Omar had honked the car horn, then walked to the gate

alongside the house at the same time that another man, in jeans and a cotton shirt, approached from the inside.

"Qué pasó, cuñado?!" Omar greeted him with genuine joy.

"Aquí nomás," the man came back less enthusiastic, but friendly enough, opening his chain-link gate. He and Omar embraced, slapping each other's back.

Mickey and Butch followed them, listening to all the long-time-no-see exchanges.

"You guys are just in time," the man said, handing them a half-emptied bottle of tequila. "I got some Jack's inside too if this don't keep us warm enough."

The wind was thrashing around unnaturally. Grits of sand either struck their eyes or came so close they had to shut them—Omar didn't seem to notice or mind, while the only complaint Fernie might have voiced was about his cap, which, about to jump off, he had to keep tugging back onto his head.

The back of the house, about an acre, was newly fenced in. Cottonwoods and pecan trees, some tamarisks near the irrigation canal, once served as a more natural boundary line between Fernie's place and his only visible neighbor, most of the other land around him being farmed. In the middle, within, was mostly dirt and flowering weeds, except that above that dirt were homemade cages for maintaining roosters, fighting cocks. With no wind, their crowing would have overpowered any sound that was not Fernie and Omar talking. Fernie, his own feathers blooming, gave Omar and Mickey and Butch the tour around, bragging on his whiteheads and redheads and Hatches and McLeans, telling them about each bird's breeding and abilities to cut and leap and endure. This new fence, Fernie told them, was to keep out thieves, either nearby kids or mejicanos, whose border was about a mile away.

Two other men, one tall and one short, both otherwise

dressed like Fernie in jeans and cotton shirts, came from deeper behind Fernie's house. They were all introduced to one another and the bottle was passed around. Then Fernie's friends selected one of the birds.

"Like I told you, you're just in time," Fernie said, his cap finally blowing free.

Mickey ran over for it. On its front was a brownheaded rooster with glossy green plumage, words above EL MERO GAL- LERO, and below, Y LO MÁS CHINGÓN. Fernie, Mickey saw, hand- ing the cap back to him, had bright blue eyes just like those Omar described Lucy as having.

The group of them were walking when Omar asked Fernie about Lucy.

"No sé, no sé, like I told you already." Fernie didn't like the subject and the wind didn't conceal this. "Take it up with my mom if you want, but not with me."

Omar said something else.

Fernie stopped walking and stood into Omar's face. "Hí que la chingada! How many times I gotta *say* it to you?"

Omar nodded his head, sad, and slumped his shoulders, guilty.

They both went on, toward an abandoned, roofless adobe, one wall almost gone, its straw and mud a lump alongside of it, the top courses of the other walls lacking sections of brick too. Bales of old yellow hay created the circumference inside, leaving a circle in the middle. There was already a rooster in a cage, a white one, with the almost-two-inch, curved needle gaffs attached to his natural spurs. Fernie and the shorter of his friends, Roberto, wrapped and tied the same-length gaffs to the redheaded bird they'd just carried from the yard.

Omar and Mickey stood in a shadow of a wall. The sun, its

bottom sunk onto the horizon, beamed a theatrical kind of light into the pit. Butch sat on a bale of hay not far from them.

"Pendejo cabrón," Omar whispered to Mickey.

Mickey immediately lost some of his passion for this cock-fight. The bottle of chilled tequila was almost finished, and though none of them was feeling any pain, Omar saying something like this with a touch less civility could alter the situation quickly.

"What is it?" Mickey asked, pissed.

"Nothing," Omar whined. "Nothing, absolutely fucking nothing."

Mickey wished this were true. "Take it easy, will you?"

"Vámonos pues," Omar said. "I wanna hit that bar."

"What bar?"

"La de su tía," he said. "You'll see. Let's go."

Fernie handed his rooster to his friend Roberto, then reached to the back of his pants for his wallet. He was drunk, more so than any of the other men. "How bout we let my, uh, my cuñado here hold the green?" he asked Luther, the taller man, who was clutching the white bird. "Whadaya say?" Luther, who spoke Spanish as well as he did English, nodded his agreement and reached into his front pocket for his cash. "It's okay with you?" Fernie asked Omar next. "A friendly bet, tú sabes."

Omar nodded unenthusiastically, but Fernie didn't notice. The two men each handed Omar five bills.

Fernie took back his bird from Roberto, and he and Luther, both cuddling the roosters against their chest, then shoulder to shoulder, bringing the birds face to face, bill to bill, to nip at each other, to know what they were there for. Ready, the two men put the birds to the dirt, and Fernie's friend Roberto called "Pit!" and the animals went into a leaping blur, crowing and clicking steel gaffs.

Fernie's bird, his red, was on top when the action slowed, a gaff stuck below the neck of the white bird. Fernie's rooster panted, his eyes defiant, when Fernie drew him off the other, and when he put him down for the next pitting, his rust hackles bloomed stiffly like a desert flower, and, mixing with his exotic, glowing olive green tail feathers, made the quickly wounded white, his dull white hackles wilted, his black tail feathers straggling in the dirt, seem a little too small, a middleweight in a heavyweight bout. Fernie's red outleaped and cut the white again, sticking another gaff into the white's breast.

"It's over, man," Mickey said to Omar.

Omar, thinking the same, reached into his front pocket to check the money.

The birds were pitted again. Already the white had trouble keeping balance.

"Mira!" Omar whispered to Mickey. He was cupping one of the bills.

"What?" Mickey asked.

"Que mires, vato!" Omar told him.

Mickey saw the bill with Ulysses S. Grant on it, a fifty.

Omar slipped his hand to his back pocket, and, dependent on the shadows to hide what he was doing, slid all the money neatly into the slot of his leather billfold, then he rearranged the holdings with his own cash.

Fernie and Luther continued to pit the birds until finally Luther conceded that his white, if not dead, was near enough.

To celebrate, Fernie lifted back the last swallow of the tequila. "Aiii!" he yelped, then he shouted at Luther, "You can make me rich any day!" Luther coughed up a laugh and shook his head.

Omar unfolded his wallet and handed Fernie the money,

which Fernie counted, his eyes focusing in and out. Two hundred dollars, 10 twenties.

"We're gone," he told a satisfied Fernie. "We're gonna check out the bar, see if . . ." Omar didn't finish.

"Andale pues," Fernie said, not caring the least.

The Hideout Lounge was a Spanish-style building in the middle of what had become, except for the stars and moon, desert blackness. The only other light was from two windows, baby blue painted shutters inside blotting most of that out, and two outside lamps aimed at the sign above the door and between the windows. Omar parked the car in a packed, hard-dirt lot surrounding it. The wind, inhaling and exhaling congestively, pushed around a distinctive odor of horseshit.

"Don't you love the smell?" Mickey said as they went in.

"You're sick, cuñado," Omar said, pulling the door open.

"I mean it," Mickey told Butch. "I really do."

Mickey and Butch took a table not far from the pool table while Omar aimed for the bar. New relative to the building, the bar was still old, its black naugahyde edge padding mended with electrician's tape, its chrome rusting. A base-to-ceiling mirror and glass liquor cabinet was its main attraction. Omar had headed straight toward the woman sitting on a stool at the corner, an ashtray with cigarette smoke ribboning near her. They embraced, and Omar greeted her stridently. The woman remained unmoved from her cushioned stool.

Mickey and Butch had ordered bottles of beer from the barmaid who came over to them.

"We better be ready tonight," Mickey told Butch.

Butch was as verbal as ever.

" 'Cuz you know that Fernie's gonna realize he gave ese pinche Omar a fifty and not a twenty. And he knows where we are right now.''

"Already Omar's too fucked up," Butch said in his whisper.

"Me too," Mickey said. "But let's play eight ball anyways." Mickey got some quarters for the small table, then found as good a cue as he could from the wall rack, dusted his hands, and chalked the tip. "Listo jalisco," he said. "My peseta breaks."

He and Butch played, and it was the same as everything else—Mickey couldn't lose, Mickey looked like he practiced for hours every day.

"I don't know what it is," Mickey confessed to Omar, who had left the woman, Lucy's aunt, who hadn't so much as uncrossed her legs. Omar dropped into a chair at the table, slouching, glum. He was drinking bourbon and water. "So you know where she is now?" Mickey finally got around to asking.

"Bitch," Omar said.

"No, en otras palabras," said Mickey.

"Fucking bitch," Omar said. "Fucking whore."

"Wha'd her aunt say?"

"Says she don't know, but she lies," said Omar, that childish tone in his voice now coming out drunken and slurred.

Mickey sank the eight ball again, and rolled his pool stick on the table. "Entonces, let's get the fuck outta here."

"I need a drink," Omar said, standing up, then stumbling over to the bar.

Butch, who'd been banking the cue ball for practice, stuck another quarter in the coin slot, and the balls rolled to one end.

"You break," Mickey told him, worried because now Omar was carrying on with two guys near Lucy's aunt, and the conversation didn't seem friendly. Mickey and Butch hadn't ordered the two beers that arrived through the barmaid.

Omar returned, a full drink with fresh fat ice cubes in his hand, the two guys next to him. "This is Louie, Fernie's brother," Omar said, introducing only the one with the Levi's jacket on. The other wore a brown leather vest and a long-sleeve shirt. Mickey raised his head a little in acknowledgment, and took the table since Butch didn't drop any on the break.

"I'm the big ones?" Mickey asked Butch.

Butch shook his head. "Cualquiera."

Louie hid a quarter on the green felt under the cushion near the coin slot to challenge the next game.

"We're probably not gonna stay," Mickey said. "You and your partner can have the table to yourselves."

"We can stay," Omar yelled.

"We can go too," Mickey told him back. "It'd be better."

"I gotta wait for Lucy a little while here," Omar said.

Nobody acted like they heard Omar, but everybody heard too well.

Mickey, after sinking a couple, missed. Then Butch came up and missed badly. It rotated like this a few turns, not like Mickey was so good, maybe only that he was so much better than Butch that he couldn't lose. And he didn't lose.

"I'll put fifty bucks on my compadre," Omar hollered from the table after Louie drove the quarter in and began dropping the balls in the triangle.

Louie grinned.

"I ain't joking," Omar said. "Fifty bucks." He slapped the U. S. Grant on the table in front of him. "Fifty bucks to burn or to earn."

Mickey couldn't believe Omar was being so obvious. He glowered at him, then at Butch for not showing any practical outrage either. "You're too drunk, man," he told Omar. "Let's get outta here."

"Orale," Louie said, after he fit and organized the last ball and then lifted the triangle up. "Break," he said to Mickey.

"I don't wanna do this," Mickey said, laying the cue on the green pool table again.

"It's a friendly bet, don't worry so much," Omar told him. "Verdad, cuñado? You won't bet what you don't got. A friendly bet."

"I already said to break," Louie acknowledged.

Mickey sighed. He picked up his pool cue. He chalked the end, then went and dusted his palms. "But after this one we go, okay?"

Omar didn't say yes.

Mickey stroked the cue ball hard because he was pissed off and too drunk himself, scattering the balls, burying the eight ball.

Omar howled and banged the table loud and obnoxiously, even knocking over Mickey's beer. "Qué pasó, cuñado?!"

Louie put in another quarter, and the three that fell in the last game came to the open end. Louie began setting the balls in the triangle. He was resolved to rematch.

"Again?" Omar asked tauntingly.

"You don't need to be a fucking culo," Louie told him.

"Yeah, settle down, Omar," Mickey agreed.

Mickey wanted to quit, but knew he'd have to play one more after this one no matter who won. Stupid images and scenes threw themselves into his vision. Mr. Crockett, mailboxes, Fred's vodka, ping-pong, McDonald's, interviews with the star of the team, Rosemary's big breasts. The man who told the story about seeing him at the restaurant. He remembered it, sort of. It *was* him. And it wasn't him who told the story. The man did. That was even more evidence that some of what happened *was* true. Now he was drinking his beer, looking around, Mexican music—guitarras, a bass, trumpets and trombones, an accordion, a sweet woman's high voice—rattling the jukebox's speaker, and he was playing pool, and Louie was right over there, waiting on him. It *was* real. As confused as he had gotten he knew that life was real too. He thought about Big Jake. Big Jake never lost his teeth when he fought. Big Jake never broke his nose in a fight. Big Jake didn't have to pay a doctor when he got cut or shot. It crossed his mind, Mickey would say, that the best thing, just as in this case, was to give it all up, move along. Because something serious was going to happen. He knew it, knew it in his bones.

"Another fifty bucks," Louie said.

"I better see it first, don't you think?" Omar told him. "You haven't put down the fifty you owe me yet."

"I'm good for it," Louie protested.

"I'm sure you are, cuñado," said Omar.

The way Omar called him cuñado this time, especially in that babyish singsong of his, tore it out openly from Louie, all over his face. He dug into his wallet and counted out fifty dollars in various denominations and tossed the cash at the table.

"Yeah, but what about this next fifty?" Omar, overly relaxed in his chair, or like that red rooster, wouldn't let up.

"I'm good for it." Louie was at the edge of snapping, and his friend seemed to be getting ready too.

"Break," Louie told Mickey. "It's your break."

Mickey blinked a few times to make himself stay in the world. Then he cracked the balls, and the small ones became his. He dropped two more, then Louie took his turn. They went back and forth. Louie had two balls left when Mickey came down to the eight ball, which was an easy straight shot across the table into the corner it was close to. Mickey lined up to take it.

"It's one bank," Louie said.

That finally stood Omar up. "Hey, when did you decide *that* rule?" Louie was a head taller, but Omar didn't act like he cared.

"It's all right," Mickey interrupted, interceding before Louie forgot about the game. "Just relax, okay?" Mickey wanted to be cautious. He angled out the shot for a couple of seconds. Of course, he couldn't lose: He gave the cue ball a just-right, soft touch against the cushion, and it homed in to bump the eight gently into its hole.

"Que la chingada madre," Louie mumbled, clenching his teeth away from the table for just a moment, then turning directly back to the coin slot.

"Wait, wait!" Omar shouted, drunk. "Money talks, bullshit walks! Let's see the cash!"

Louie's friend, from the other table, moved toward Omar. Mickey saw Butch stand, his dark brown head looking hard and mean and bad, but as difficult to fully see as his voice was to hear. It was the first time Mickey'd ever seen Butch show any aggression.

Louie's mother, Lucy's aunt, rushed over to kick the unwelcomed ones out. Louie calmed her.

"Cálmela también, hombre," Mickey suggested to Omar.

"I want my money," Omar said, boasting at Lucy's aunt, "and I don't think the dude's got it."

"You'll get your money," Louie told him, bobbing his head nervously.

Now even Mickey was feeling excited. "You good for this bet, man?"

"Yeah I'm good for it, like I said already."

"Tonight? Like right now?"

He nodded his head angrily, carefully eyeballing various sections of Mickey's face.

Mickey didn't believe him for a second, but thought Omar, everybody, was so drunk he could lose and nobody'd notice.

"He loses, he owes me a hundred bucks!" Omar shouted.

"You got a hundred bucks, man?" Mickey asked.

Louie nodded. "Break."

"But this is la ultima. Right?" A rhetorical question, Mickey checked it with both Louie and Omar.

Mickey swatted the rack with the cue ball. The balls spread out poorly but Mickey was still able, after one had fallen on the break, to get another small one. Then the two traded misses, back and forth until Louie got a run, his cue ball resting right where he wanted it to each time. Mickey had four left, and Louie had two when he went after one of his solids in the side pocket. It struck where he aimed, but too hard, and when the cue ball caromed off, it tapped one of Mickey's striped ones, then ticked the eight ball, which rolled into the corner pocket. The cue ball died in a perfect line for what would have been Louie's last two easy shots.

Louie halved his stick against the table.

"That's one hundred bucks, maricón!" Omar shouted disrespectfully, rocking unsteadily on his feet the whole time. "Let's have it!"

"Fuck you!" Louie screamed. He held the taco, the pool cue, in his hand as a weapon. "Get the fuck outta here before I hurt your fat ass!"

Louie's friend came into the light too, a buck knife locked open, and got close to Omar.

"We'll go!" Mickey said. "Just let us go, all right?"

Omar backed away from the knife, went wide around Louie, and back-stepped toward the door. Mickey was already close to it, even with Louie a few steps in front of him. Mickey held onto his pool stick.

But nobody had paid any attention to Butch, who was behind the guy with the knife, out of the light. Butch was catlike in his walk, and, without a flinch of expression, sucker-punched Louie's buddy across the face with a long-neck beer bottle. The dude never anticipated it, nobody would have.

And as though it were a practiced next move, Mickey drove his boot into Louie's nuts the second Louie gaped at his friend— turned his head—and then Mickey did it again, as effectively the second time with Louie's hands there as the first time without.

And Omar, Mickey, and Butch carefully backed out the front door of the Hideout Lounge, Mickey still with a pool stick in his hand, and, once on the other side of the door, hauled ass to Omar's Nova.

"Que pasen buenas noches," Butch said at his open window from the backseat as Omar started the car. It was as boisterous and loud a sentence as had ever been heard from him.

"What?" Mickey asked him, surprised not only by the sarcasm but that he could hear it so well.

Butch's smile was about as loud as a laugh.

"Should I drive?" Mickey asked the drunken Omar.

Omar didn't answer, maybe didn't hear, and it was too late anyway. The Nova's tires spit rocks and dust around the dirt parking lot and Omar squealed the car onto the asphalt road and the three men drove away into the darkness of the Wild West.

Mickey opened the window and the yellow curtains and stretched out on his springy bed, the sudden absence of wind haunting. Then he heard something else. So distant it was almost imperceptible. Like someone's name he couldn't remember, or the melody of a song—it was right there on the tip of his tongue.

He squeezed his mind but couldn't get it. So much like this, so much like a memory. Unless it was not memory he was listening to, digging for.

Mickey wanted to understand what was real. When did it start? How did he end up like this, end up here at the Y?

Better to forget. And so he tried to forget. Unless it was not memory, and forgetting wasn't right.

A train so faraway still that it was like the call of a storm as it approached or was skirting by. Mickey heard it until it came to a stop.

Then so quiet again he had to hear the man across from him begin farting.

He needed sleep.

He closed his eyes.

Roosters crowed in his head, their fighting screech embedded like stains of blood on a white shirt.

The top of his foot, where it drove between Louie's legs, throbbed.

None of that happened?

He needed to be asleep. Really he hates this. Really. But there it comes. He sees it and listens.

A ball goes in, bounce pass back. Going, coming. In, back.

"He's just so strong, and I don't even think he's realized all his talent yet."

"I don't agree. Okay, he's having a good season, a great one even. Lots of guys do, but he's also on a great team that backs him up. Without it . . ."

"Gimme a break! How can you say that? He *is* the team."

"I'm sorry. No. *Helps.* You know I'm not saying he's not a real good player. But you shouldn't overrate him either. It cheapens everything. You can't tell me he's *that* good."

"Yes, that's exactly what I can tell you! Hey, I think he's better than good. Not only that, you wait, he's getting better."

"So easy to say that."

"What's it gonna take? Does his team win, does he score lots?"

Pass in, over to, then to, back to, then he gets it, great defense but he does it, and he jumps back in position, he's ready. Play goes on. He does do it, takes it in. Watch! Oh! The two who were talking are still. Then one of them is shutting up, the other one is going. "Look!" he says. The ball moves, goes—there!

Mickey woke up to a pounding at the door. Still mostly asleep, he thought it might be Isabel, the maid. Then he realized this wasn't her method of announcing her presence. It was the Sarge. Mickey opened the door and got back in bed with his jeans on.

"What happened?" the Sarge demanded to know.

Mickey rubbed his eyes. Already he couldn't be a hundred percent sure about what happened at the bar—it didn't seem real. More like a story from a cheap western. Or one he'd tell and be asking himself whether it really occurred or not. He was sure the Sarge wouldn't believe it. "Like I been telling you, Sarge, it's cowboys and Indians out there."

As usual, the Sarge didn't seem to approve. "I waited for you at the court. I didn't find you in the pool either."

Mickey had to look up. The Sarge was standing there, expecting a justification like a boss about being real late for work. Or worse than that, because he wasn't only irritated but disappointed too.

"What time is it?" Mickey asked.

"Past lunch," he said.

Mickey had missed doing his regular workout and missed this scheduled handball game—Monday, Wednesday, Friday—with the Sarge. It was, once he gave it an extra thought, the first time since they'd been playing that he'd missed a date.

"I guess I fucked up," Mickey said, meaning really that he *got* fucked up.

"I guess so," the Sarge said seriously.

"Guilty as charged." Mickey couldn't miss picking up on the gravity of the Sarge's attitude—hurt, or like he'd lost respect for him—and Mickey was embarrassed by it, felt awkward. "I'll make it up to you, promise," he said, trying not to sound insincere. "If that's okay?" He couldn't imagine how the Sarge was going to answer.

"You probably better get going so you can eat and go to work," the Sarge said.

"Absolutely," Mickey agreed.

At first Mickey thought Rosemary might be doing a tease to benefit and torment Oscar, who she flirted with all the time. But she'd gotten intimate enough with Mickey that he didn't think she was faking. Unless he was misinterpreting this pushing of her breasts against him. Though he found this distraction she offered agreeable enough, he worried about the opinion of her mother, who was working by herself in the office room behind the desk, very nearby, who Rosemary was supposed to be helping out. And though Mrs. Schweitz either wasn't saying or didn't notice or really didn't care, Mickey had to be practical. He did want this job—he needed this money until it was time for him to leave; it was the only money he had—and so he tried to act like he wasn't enjoying it, or, at least within plain sight, like he wasn't fondling her in return.

Oscar was smiling longingly, the weight of Rosemary's breasts against him vicariously.

"Whadaya think, Oscar?" Mickey asked. He really kind of meant it.

"Sí, Oscar, qué piensas tú?" Rosemary asked him with a terrible accent, pushing her glands more securely against Mickey.

Oscar shook his head, still with a smile, though a bittersweet one.

"Te gusta swimming, Oscar?" Rosemary asked. "Mickey looks *bueno* when he swims." She snuggled against him more. "Do you look good too?" Rosemary had watched Mickey swimming on a couple of mornings she'd brought her mother to work.

Oscar slapped the formica at and in the usual spot, but not with his regular spirit. He was taking off because he couldn't stand it. Sad and jealous, he was moving on to what he was paid for.

"Back to it!" Mickey said anyway. He did feel sorry for Oscar. Though he also felt sorry for the Sarge whenever he beat the shit out of him at handball. Things work out how they work out. Nothing is unintentional. Besides, Mickey really did *need,* and a large breast poking his arm and shoulder, even sheathed, made him feel male again.

Oscar's attitude even helped heighten her value to Mickey, not only as an object of competition, which had to have some kind of worth, but because Mickey believed that Oscar, being older and wiser, should know more about love passed up and regretted later. Hadn't Mickey only lost opportunities? What kind of female—if one ever again at all, he worried—might be next? It was only when Oscar left the scene that Omar's observations soured the offerings—Rosemary was awful unattractive. Though from a distance she wasn't so bad, and maybe up real close she might be okay too, and anyway only they would know. In between, in average conversation space between people, Mickey might have to yield to the ugly facts about Rosemary. Aside from pimples and the dark brown roots at the base of her bleached blond hair—these could be taken care of—she was Mrs. Schweitz's daughter who had inherited Mrs. Schweitz's face: a nose somewhat blunted and pug, cheeks naturally pink and plump, a mouth with a less than delicate span. And, though her breasts were conspicuously female, and though she had waist, hips, legs, apparently all the basic goodies, none of them could be magazine winners either. Nevertheless. And nevertheless. And besides, there were moments when he really thought she wasn't that bad. And who was he?

"I told my boyfriend about you," she said coquettishly after Mickey had punched some number and alphabet keys on the register, took money, made change, and said thank you.

Mickey was surprised. It was the first he'd heard of him. "Boyfriend, huh? And wha'd you tell him?"

"I told him about you. About us."

"Wha'd you tell him about me? About us?"

"Just stuff," she said. She'd wedged herself between the edge of the counter and Mickey, who was on the stool, and was able to aim her breasts into Mickey's left side at will, though with some unrelated pretense: With no one around besides her mother, who was behind the two of them and consumed by her work, right then it was to pick fuzzballs off his shirt.

"Just stuff? What stuff?"

"Well, like that you've been over to my house."

"Why would you tell him that?" It was pretty obvious, and Mickey really wondered what she was telling him for.

"You could come over. Why don't you come over?"

"You never asked."

"Well why don't you?"

" 'Cuz you never asked."

"Well, I'm asking."

"Sure, I'll come over. You know it's gonna be okay?" Mickey nodded his head and eyes a little toward where Mrs. Schweitz worked.

"Mom," Rosemary said, trying to shove her sternum into Mickey's shoulder and thus squeezing a different breast against each side. "We can make dinner for Mickey, can't we?"

Mickey feared looking back, moving at all, but heard, finally, Mrs. Schweitz.

"Certainly," she said. "It'd be our pleasure."

"See?" said Rosemary.

"But what's your boyfriend gonna say?"

She held her finger to her lips, wiggling her eyes toward her mother. "He must already know, don't you think?" She laughed. "He's not from here," she went on, whispering.

"You mean he doesn't live here?"

"No, I mean he's a GI. He's stationed at Fort Bliss. My mom doesn't like him."

"Why's that?"

"Well, my mom says he's crazy," she confided. She concentrated on the fuzzballs.

"So go on."

"He's insanely protective of me, and insanely jealous."

Mickey couldn't tell if Rosemary was playing. "Really?"

"One time he did threaten Mr. Fuller." She waited a few seconds. "He thought Mr. Fuller tried to put the make on me." She waited a few seconds again. "I told him he did because Mr. Fuller threatened to fire my mom and it made me mad." She waited again. "It wasn't exactly a lie anyway."

"So that's why your mom doesn't like him?"

Rosemary leaned very close to Mickey's ear because Mrs. Schweitz was moving around, getting her things ready to leave. "Well, he might be dangerous. She might be right."

They left and Mickey had to punch lots of the number and alphabet keys again during the rush hours of everyone else's after-work exercise.

John Hooper slammed a fist into the counter. "What's news in the nuthouse?"

"Not much," Mickey said, not sure what to say.

"No news is good news," said John Hooper.

"You said it," said Mickey.

"Take her easy now," John Hooper said. "Don't let 'em take you without a fight."

Mickey was in Omar's room and they were smoking a joint. The two of them had lost track of Butch. A first.

"You hear that the Sarge smokes it?" Mickey asked.

Omar shook his head, dismissing the idea. Omar had become miserably sad and gloomy. Mickey, meanwhile, was uneasy even thinking about Lucy, let alone trying to discuss this mystery of her, so the obvious conversation was the one most avoided.

"I never smoked it with him," Mickey said with conviction, defensively, "but I saw the bag of weed, that's true."

"I don't know about you," Omar told him.

Even if he felt sorry for him, Mickey wasn't sympathetic enough to be insulted. "There's lotsa things I suppose you don't believe that're true."

Omar ignored him to the point of not listening. "This ain't gonna cut it," Omar said, changing the subject completely.

Mickey wouldn't let the subject be changed. "I probably

shouldn't have told you any of that stuff. But you wait. You'll see what I'm talking about. If no real bad bullshit happens, I'm gonna show you the money." If he'd tiptoed around it before, he stomped now. He danced the floor poorly around Omar.

"The guy's kinda weird," Omar said offhandedly, still not responding to Mickey's story. "Into dirty magazines serious."

"Who is?"

"Sarge."

"How do you know *that?*"

"I just know."

"Yeah but how do you know?" Omar was being too enigmatic and Mickey didn't like it anymore.

"I heard a story."

"Por qué me chingas, cabrón? You gonna say it or what? Quit fucking around!"

"I just heard a story is all." Omar nearly left it there. "A dude in the coffee shop told us how Sarge got stopped crossing the border with piles of them and he had all this trouble. Transporting pornography. The Sarge called your big-eared boss dude to help him get his car back. They got something going or something like that."

Mickey let the weed float the conspiracy a few seconds. "Man, this place is a nuthouse, ain't it? Hard to believe about Mr. Straight and Narrow. What next, you know what I mean?"

Omar combined an exhale with a sigh. "This ain't gonna cut it," he repeated, "it ain't gonna cut it no more." He started digging through the clothes he had laying around.

"You know, the Sarge has been real nice to me since I been here," Mickey pondered out loud, "but lately he's been seeming pretty strange. "In lotsa ways he is normal too. He just takes normal to new heights. I ever tell you about him beating off at night?"

That caught Omar off guard and he nearly choked on a laugh.

"No shit," Mickey said, laughing too.

"How you know about him beating off if you're not with him?!" Omar squealed harder with the thought.

"It's that the guy has the room next to me, you know, and sometimes I hear the bed thumping against the wall. He humps his mattress like he's on top of a woman!"

Omar howled in tears and Mickey got caught up in it too. They laughed like that until it was out of them.

"Fuck," said Omar. "That almost made me feel better."

"We need some whiskey, or some beer at least," said Mickey.

"A lo menos," said Omar.

"Or a woman. We need some *womans*." Mickey knew better than to confess it to Omar, but his private images were of Rosemary.

Women weren't the best topic for Omar. "You want one of these?" He held out a pill in the palm of his hand. He'd already lobbed one on his tongue, then searched and found a warm, opened can of soda sitting on his YMCA room desk.

"Qué es?"

"Dilaudid." Omar swallowed and made a face. "Fucking ashes in there!" he said, almost crushing the can as he put it back on the desk, though not throwing it in the trash. "Got 'em today."

Mickey shook his head. "It's not prescription, verdad?" Mickey knew what the drug was.

"N'hombre," Omar said. "Puro street. Long time ago I used to cook it once in a while. Fact, if I had the gear . . ." He didn't go on.

Mickey turned it down, and, now with Sarge in his mind, didn't like it.

"It feels so good," Omar explained, "I gotta be careful. You know?"

Mickey started thinking about what Omar's problems with Lucy were. He'd never said, and Mickey, as was his custom, didn't ask.

"You sure?" Omar asked again.

"No," Mickey told him. "But I won't anyways."

Omar put the pill offered to Mickey back in an aspirin jar. "Cools me out."

Mickey, sitting on the edge of the bed, shook his head and looked down. He was afraid to let up, afraid everything would break loose if he did.

Omar took back the desk chair, stretched his legs.

"Can't believe what you said about the Sarge," Mickey said after what seemed a long time. "I'm gonna ask Rosemary what she knows. She knows a lot about Big Ears."

"Está fea la ruca," Omar told him. "Big y ugly. I wish you coulda seen Lucy. Hijolá, you'd wanna make babies all night and the next day too!" The words he used were stronger than they came out. Omar was already feeling better, more calmly distant. Then he came back, right in front of Mickey's face. "So what happened with your other squeezies? That religious one, and the one from Juárez? What happened to her?"

"I dunno," Mickey said. "Just haven't gone to see her for a while."

Omar stared Mickey down the eyes with a small smirk.

It was timeless in the halls, on the ever-waxed linoleum floor. It could be any time of day or night—the bulb light always created mirages, puddles of gloss at the same angles—and the temperature never varied. Mickey was walking back to room 412 because he'd been to the bathroom, and as he came out across the hall, his neighbor, in striped boxers and black socks and a limp white T-shirt, his legs and arms as pale and hairless as overboiled chicken, was moving stiff-legged toward the communal bathroom with the jar of piss in his right hand. He was scuffing energetically down the hall, but his gaze shifted downwards once he saw Mickey coming straight at him—like he was counting out a few tiles in front of him.

"Qué pasó?" Mickey said, friendly like an employee, and though loud, not intentionally loud in the cool vacuum of the hall, not meaning to be so loud that it echoed.

The old guy froze up like he hadn't been spoken to in years in English or Spanish, which seemed possible. Not sure what else to do, the man slowed to almost a stop and was about to respond when, from down the hall, the cussing old guy, who was coming out of his room, roared, "Fucking shit!"

The bottle of piss shattered on the hard floor, and then, an instant after, this old man farted. He didn't jump away, didn't twitch, and so his socks soaked in the urine that laked up around his feet.

"You gotta back up, away from the broken glass!" Mickey had to tell him.

The old man could not.

"Okay then, just don't step forward," Mickey said.

The old man's thinning, uncombed hair was not all gray or white, was still holding on to the color of his better days. The old man did not take a step forward or back or even to the side. He did not move.

"Don't worry about it, okay?" Mickey said. He was wearing shoes and so he stepped into the piss and glass and grabbed hold of the old guy's arm. "I'll call one of the janitors. It's no big deal, really." Mickey guided the man, shaken and humiliated, back toward his room. At first resistant, the old man gave in, gave in so much that Mickey felt like he was carrying the man, was afraid gripping too hard might break the fragile skeleton of this man he'd never before spoken to.

Mickey won all games of the set: 21–15, 21–19, 21–13. Even the second game score wasn't really as close as it sounded. Like Omar, the Sarge had turned glum. It might not have made it any better that his fat friend Philip had watched them from the viewing area above the court.

They headed for the Burger King instead of his favorite, Mac's, because the Sarge had clipped out coupons for there. He had enough coupons for each of them, and they had to be used by this date, the expiration date.

"I was sorta surprised," Philip said. He was sitting shotgun while Mickey had the backseat. The muzak was the Carpenters. "I thought Elias would dominate." He rolled down the window, but the Sarge, saying nothing, scrolled it back up from his side's master control panel. "I'm sorry," Philip said, flashing a guilty face at the Sarge—he still drove like he was wearing satin pajamas and a velvet smoking jacket. "I've seen you play other guys before, Elias, and I really thought, well, you'd dominate." He shifted his bulk to twist his head toward the backseat and Mickey. "I don't mean anything against you, you know. Because you were great. You played real well. You had to, to beat Elias. I've seen him play before." He got himself comfortable again facing forward. "But it was great to watch, real great competition, real good games."

"So how is it you know each other?" Mickey asked.

"I lived at the Y for a while," Philip said. "In the room you have now. That's how we met."

"Coincidence," Mickey said.

"Yeah. Though you knew the guy who was staying there before me pretty good too, right, Elias?"

The Sarge nodded.

"I remember meeting him," said Philip. "Remember that time? We went out to lunch together too."

"A regular tradition, passed from generation to generation," said Mickey.

Philip laughed with his body. "That's a pretty good one, don't you think, Elias?"

The Sarge didn't respond verbally, but he didn't seem too disturbed either. He was more upset about his losing at handball.

"We used to go out with him too," Phillip told Mickey. "You'd go out with him a lot, didn't you, Elias?"

"I don't know if it was a lot."

"He said," said Mickey.

"What's that supposed to mean?"

"Means nothing," said Mickey. "I dunno what I mean. Whada you mean?"

The Sarge was even more disturbed about it, but was restraining himself.

They removed themselves from the burgundy interior and tinted windows of the car, crossing beneath the clear blue sky and golden sun, to the exact muzak station—remade Neil Diamond—inside.

"At least the burgers are different here," Mickey said, searching the ceiling for speakers.

The Sarge was distributing the coupons. "I happen to like this music."

"No shit," Mickey told him. "Hey, but I wasn't meaning offense."

They got their food on rubbery plastic trays, imitations of the hard plastic kind from the good ole days. The coupons were two Whopper burgers for one, large fries, and a medium coke. Philip ordered an extra burger and fries.

Mickey raised his paper soda cup for a toast. "Thanks for bringing me, and thanks for the coupon."

"Hear! Hear!" said Philip, raising his soda too.

"You're both welcome," the Sarge mouthed. His response might be interpreted as serious and sincere. It wasn't, though. He was self-absorbed.

"May your next neighbors carry on the tradition too!" Philip went on, chortling.

The Sarge lowered his head and went after his food—like he didn't care, or didn't want it to seem so.

"Hear hear," Mickey said, watching the Sarge's reaction carefully.

Reverend Miller approached the desk exposing his over-sized, pearly white incisors, his eyeballs seeming less swollen than before. He leaned against the counter and, as though to protect a private, intimate secret, those cloudy-sky eyes jerked about for meddling ears. "We're still waiting on that mail of mine," he told Mickey, winking. "Any hope we'll find it?"

The subject had begun to shake Mickey, and he also did not like this guy whatsoever. "It got lost or something?"

"I haven't received it yet."

"You mean they lost it?" Mickey asked. "Someone told you that?"

"They *haven't* told me yet," said the reverend, sensing a conspiracy.

"You talked to . . . well, like Fred?"

"Fred?"

"The man whose shift is before mine," Mickey explained.

"Okay. Yes. Yes I do, every day I have, and he didn't tell me."

Mickey's head swayed, confused and nervous. The Reverend Miller not only didn't seem altogether right, but his disturbance seemed bad, as in dangerous. On the other hand, and Mickey was conscious of how impractical this was, Mickey couldn't allow himself to be cooperative either.

"He didn't tell you what?" he asked, irritated. He thought about it a second more, getting more contentious. "He didn't *tell you* 'cuz it ain't *there*. You see? He can't tell you they lost what they didn't lose." His own sentences made him dizzy.

"Maybe they've put it away," the reverend said, attempting to maintain what he seemed to think was a courtliness.

Mickey laughed darkly.

"Why don't you take a peek for me?" the reverend continued, resisting that urge of his to wink. "Maybe it's in the office back there."

"They don't keep the resident mail back there," Mickey said impatiently.

"Wouldn't you please do a check for me?" The reverend used polite words but he had become threatening, the veins in his neck rising prominently, his jaws clenching, and his crazy eyes rubbing together, beginning to throw out sparks.

"Okay, all right," Mickey said standing up, angry now, and also challenged. "I'm gonna go take a look just for you, okay? Would that be good?"

"Thank you," said Reverend Miller.

Mickey backed into Mrs. Schweitz's office and shuffled through papers on the desk, then riffled a stack of letters addressed to the YMCA that had already been slit neatly by a letter opener.

"Nothing," he spoke up from there, holding those letters in his hand. He tossed them down again, returned to the front desk. "Nothing, man. Not one thing for you." He plopped back on the stool to indicate that he was through with this search, and shook his head toward Oscar, who had come around the corner. Omar was stepping out from the elevator as well, and John Hooper pushed open the glass front doors.

The Reverend Miller's fire was kindling. "I know I have mail."

Mickey raised his eyebrows and forehead, not even outwardly pretending sympathy.

Suddenly the reverend blazed, slamming both fists on the formica counter, kicking beneath the counter, punching a hole in the thin plywood and paneling. Then he raged over at the cigarette machine and, with the back of his boot heels, dented the aluminum several times.

John Hooper, Omar, Oscar, and Mickey watched from four cardinal points around the Reverend Miller, each doing nothing else but observing, motionless, afraid, but ready to defend themselves.

"Why won't you give it to me?!" the reverend screamed into Mickey's face. He pounded the desk with both fists again. "I should COME OVER there!"

Mickey was backing up gradually, very slowly, his eye out for a weapon he could use if he had to. Like encountering a wild animal, he didn't want to move in a threatening way and force an attack.

Just as abruptly the Reverend Miller whipped around toward

the front doors and with both his palms slapped them open—and was gone.

Oscar leaned into his personal station at the front desk. "Muy muy loco," he said, sounding it out more than he did normally.

"A fucking nuthouse," said John Hooper, taking off his cowboy hat to fiddle with the brim. Enough said, he disappeared into the elevator, shaking his head, disgusted by the whole affair.

"That was pretty hairy," Mickey said, his heart still thrashing.

"You know I met a guy like that once," Omar said in a style of voice as serious as anyone heard from Omar. "I'm telling you this, me entiendes? I met this dude like him once. You see how this dude looked? All tight like that? Poes, you better not try to fuck him over with anything but a bullet. Me entiendes? This dude I met, there in L.A., he was with Charlie Manson. You see lo que te dije, right? Scared the shit outta me, cuñado, I'm telling you."

Mickey started looking underneath in the shelves of the desk cabinet for something to use as a weapon.

"You mean they got no gun back there?" Omar asked.

"No creo yo," Oscar said. He didn't like the idea.

"I don't think so either," Mickey said.

"You know who does?" said Omar. "Mr. Charleston. Charles. He told us."

"Really?" That might have aroused Mickey more but he was distracted with searching the desk. He found a hammer. "This ain't better than a pistola, but if the worshipful reverend comes back, it'll fuck him up." Mickey weighed it in his hand, then put it back underneath for easy access. "I'll be ready if he does."

"Ya no tiene llave aquí," Oscar told him, insistent, not liking the violent talk. "He didn't pay, and they make him leave yesterday."

"No shit?" Mickey said.

Oscar nodded his head, then moved on to finish his chores.

After a while the Sarge had come down. Butch, of course, was there by then too.

"I wonder what it is about the mail?" Mickey said. "What if somebody did take his mail? What if somebody was doing that?"

"What would anybody want with it?" Omar asked, impatient with the idea, with Mickey's own story.

Mickey didn't want to get in an argument with Omar right there.

"It's no reason to lose control like that anyway," said the Sarge. He'd already heard all the details concerning the incident.

"Charles worries about the same thing," Mickey said. "Thinks he should have some mail that ain't here."

"Everybody knows about Charles," Omar said.

"Charles is all right," Mickey said in his defense. "Even if he does want to be a secret agent when he grows up."

The guys looked at him.

"No shit. He told me."

Only the Sarge didn't get a kick out of this information. The Sarge alone seemed sorry for Charles.

"Look, don't joke with him about it, okay? Like I say, he's all right. He's harmless, even if he's got some troubles. He's good people."

"He don't like to lose at ping-pong," Butch said, offering up another rare, audible comment.

"One thing for sure," Mickey thought to add before he forgot. "Don't say nothing to Charles about this thing with the reverend being about the mail. The poor guy would lose it for sure."

"He's gonna find out," Omar assured him.

"Yeah," Mickey sighed. "Probably so. I still hope not."

*   *   *

It was an afternoon as colorful and warm as a Mexican blanket and Omar wanted to go out, so he and Mickey drove up the river valley and pulled off the old, abandoned highway at a restaurant-bar painted the same dirty pink as a desert sunset. They ate just-steamed tamales and sipped cold beer and shot pool. And all on Omar, who was unusually buoyant and peaceful. The bar itself was gaudy with windows and light, with ristras of dried red chile and strings of elephant-sized garlic for sale, with a hall of large and small photographs of sons and daughters, mothers and fathers, grandfathers and grandmothers, grandsons and grand-daughters, in-laws, godparents, aunts and uncles and cousins, friends and good customers.

"I'm gonna give Butch the car," said Omar, whose speech today was especially enunciated and melodic in that childish tone he had. Butch was back in the glass booth of his gas station job, unable to take the drive. "No vale madre, really, and, you know, he's got kids."

"I didn't know that," said Mickey. It might not have been his dream car, but it was a car, and he was disappointed.

"Three of them."

"He never said shit to me." Mickey had just won another game of pool, the fourth in a row.

"You should make your living at this, cuñado," Omar told him, pushing in another quarter.

"It's pure luck."

"Orale vato, pura suerte."

"Honest. I can't explain it." Mickey smiled. He wasn't ashamed of this new talent, this winning, it was true, and he was beginning to have moments when he thought maybe . . . well, like

even, after all this time, that money would come just like he
wanted, he'd be able to move on, he could afford to live, he could
get a car, all that he thought about. That the winning was a sign
of some kind. "Really."

"Pásame algo pues," Omar said. "I need some of that shit
bad."

"So what's the plan with you?"

"To book out of this one-horse town."

"So you quit?" Mickey asked him again. He thought it more
likely that Omar'd been fired.

"Gave 'em notice at the end of the day."

"Pero, no problems there or nothing?"

"Peace on earth, goodwill to man."

"Is that the street name for it these days?"

Omar didn't recognize that. He missed his shot. "Did I tell
you about the other night?" he said. "It's one of the reasons I think
my time is up here."

"Which other night?" Mickey asked.

"That I was with these dudes. You tell me what you think."
Omar took a measured amount of time as Mickey sank two more
of his before a miss. He wouldn't step up to take his turn. Mickey
couldn't read whether this was going to be a joke story or serious
because Omar didn't treat the two differently—he stood awkwardly still, both hands sliding up and down the narrow end of a
pool cue.

"The other night I was out with these dudes from work. One
dude really, and some other vatos he knew. We got all fucked up,
you know? All fucked up. We drove someplace, I dunno where.
Nowhere, the middle of a nowhere it was like. Cactus and dirt and
weeds that stick to you and get stuck all over your threads. I was

all fucked up. Me entiendes? It was dark, dark like a bad dream. You know? Like this smoke in the air. Black as it was, all these stars were above, still up there like you was on a planet in space. But we were in an arroyo, there were mountains right over there and rocks all around, and the smoke was so thick, you could smell the color of it. Gray and brown. Gray from burning tires and brown from wood. You couldn't see where it was coming from, it was just everywhere, like it *was* the air. So these dudes started a fire in the dirt. A big fire. Big and tall flames. And then I started feeling crazy, like all these dudes was after me. You got what I mean? I got *freaked* 'cuz there was too many of them. And I don't get scared like that, me entiendes? But I did, I got big-time scared, like I might water my pants. I'm telling you. You know? I kept on telling myself I was crazy. But then there was this one dude and he pulled out a shank. A bad shank, cuñado, I'm telling you, like *this* long. I was freaked, I was sure it was gonna all come down, like the devil. I didn't know where the fuck I was, and who were all these pendejos, and I kept on hearing that fire, sucking and sizzling. You listen to that fire before, cuñado?"

Omar stopped talking and drank from his can of beer. But even after he had digested it he didn't go on. He eyeballed the lay of the pool table as though it were all that was left to do.

"So?" Mickey pushed it.

"Es todo," Omar told him. It seemed like he'd gotten tired, not that there wasn't more to tell. "I just wondered what you'd think."

Mickey shook his head. "I don't think nothing yet, man," said Mickey. "I don't think I do anyway. I'm not sure I get it."

Omar lined out a shot geometrically, staring down the length of his stick.

"But nothing happened to you, right?" Mickey asked, clueless about what he was expected to extract from the incident. "I mean, you got home, and nobody fucked you up. Right?"

Omar missed his shot. He shook his head as clearly as he'd spoken.

"I guess I don't get it," Mickey mumbled. He finished off the game, banking in the eight ball. He felt a little bad because he thought he must have missed something, whatever it was.

"You're all right," Omar told him.

"I hear you're all right, too," Mickey told him back.

They both decided to leave and they got back in the Nova and drove.

"I'd give my son the car if I could."

"You got a son?"

"Almost twenty years old."

"No!"

"For reals," Omar said. "I jumped outta school when I was thirteen 'cuz I was in love. Me and his moms, she was only twelve, and we never looked back. A real stupid romance. I was a dumb chavalito. I got into bikes, rode, did a lotta shit. So that's why I gotta give este carro to Butch 'cuz one day we ain't never gonna see him again, and he's gotta get one of the breaks. I picked up a trade and got union in Califas, but pinche Butch's got nothing aquí en este pinche Tejas."

He didn't like it, and he didn't go around asking for handouts, still he wondered why Omar wouldn't help him out like he was Butch. Was this a form of compliment? He needed a car too. He thought about having a car a lot, right? But he didn't bring the subject up. Not directly.

"Pretty soon I'm gonna move along too, get outta that fucking YMCA room. I'm barely making it right now, but I don't want another one of those fucking jobs I got before, for some hick shitkicker. If that money comes," Mickey said, making his story as true sounding as possible, "or even if it don't." Mickey listened to and felt the air brushing his hair as they rode, brown desert dirt on either side of them. Then he decided to speak up again. "I know you don't believe me, Omar, but what I been telling you is true. It makes me feel shitty because somebody like you don't believe me. It's that I can't talk about it, about all of it, even to people I trust. It's just not how it oughta be done. It wouldn't be right, it wouldn't be smart. I wish I'd never mentioned it."

Omar kept a pause between them. "Don't worry about it," he said.

That didn't go far enough to satisfy Mickey. "One last thing," he said, wanting to sound absolutely certain. "It's only that somebody could get hurt. I know how you don't believe me . . . but I'm telling you somebody might want me fucked over, I ain't shitting you."

"Outlaw stuff," Omar came right back. "The Wild West."

"Well," said Mickey, hopeful that he might finally have reached Omar, even if he had to ignore the sarcasm in Omar's tone. "Kind of."

The road was blue sky above and wooden electrical poles below, wires draping parallel and perpendicular, and sometimes plowed field, sometimes unplowed creosote and mesquite, salt-bush and Indian grass. And then beyond and rising above some tall gnarled cottonwoods clumped with slime-green mistletoe was a taller white Spanish façade, fortresslike. Omar wheeled toward the monument like this were his intention all along.

At the highest point of the mission front, at the top of a bell tower, was a huge iron crucifix. Three bells in descending sizes were below, where pigeons and doves made their home. Inside, carved, fat vigas spanned the width of the high ceiling, holding what seemed like a lightweight Indian thatching. Its walls were adobe, three or four feet thick, some of it crumbling at the base, its plaster gone, waterlogged by the poor drainage during summer monsoons and winter. The pews were so old they were dark brown with a thick, waxy substance that must have stayed under the nails of those who carved their names into their backs.

Both Omar and Mickey had, out of respect, folded their dark glasses once they'd opened the heavy wooden doors. Omar approached the holy water solemnly, touched his fingers to it, crossed himself and kneeled, dabbing his black T-shirt with the sacred liquid. The holy room was blue and green and red with the light generated from the stained glass windows, and the bouquets of still fresh flowers on a table in front of the main altar mixed their bloom with the incense the fathers used to purify and sanctify two hundred years of masses in the mission. Behind the main altar was the crucified Christ, emaciated, the flesh at his elbows and knees ripped open, the wounds white with depth, while his feet and hands were nailed, the blood thick and coagulated. His head, a crown of harsh desert thorns cutting his skin, its blood dripping down to his shoulders and chest and thighs; his head, eyes open, aimed skyward, sad and begging, imploring.

Off to the side of the main altar, in an alcove, was an image of the Holy Mother, the Virgin, the serene mother, draped so warm in a luxurious green shawl with heaven's stars embroidered in it, her dark hands clasping a red rose. She stood in front of a golden yucca, its sharp, needle-pointed leaves bright like rays of the sun. Beneath her was the child Juan Diego, holding her up with his arms and shoulders—though his body, like a gray boulder underneath the Virgin, had coarse, mean gray horns, making the little boy seem as strong as a bull made of stone.

Omar kneeled awkwardly at the altar in front of La Virgin Maria de Guadalupe and, with his whole arm, waved Mickey over to do the same. Omar reached into his pocket and dug out a crumpled ten-dollar bill and a handful of change.

"You got anything?" he asked Mickey, his breath soaked in beer.

"A little is all," Mickey said.

"Echalo," Omar demanded, finding a wooden match near the display of votives. He lit a candle. "You see, we gotta leave everything in this church. We gotta say, 'Holy Mother and God, we need some help, we're going through a trip and we need the help.' Even if it's your last dollar you gotta do it, cuñado, you gotta say, 'God, I'm gonna give you my last dollar!' And even if it is your last and only bola, you gotta do it. Even if you're starving and you could buy some eats, you give it to Her anyways. Even if the priest looks like a fat-pig wino, cuñado, 'cuz it don't matter where it goes and how it gets there, once it leaves la mano it finds God and He knows what you done. So that's what you gotta do, that's what we gotta do. Por eso I just gave him todo el money I got. Now you put it in there too, me entiendes, cuñado?"

Mickey was worried about Omar—he was not understanding much of the day's events—and worried about how much gas was in the car, but, in the spirit of the moment, he reached down in his pocket and found some coins. He also felt two dollar bills he had but left them where they were. He dropped the change in the tin vegetable can for donations and he lit a candle too. And then Mickey did pray for himself. It took him some time to get his thoughts straight because he had so many and they were all so confusing. But then it came out simple: Please help me to get through this, please don't let me die.

They gave the candles enough silent time to melt a small

Dagoberto Gilb

circle around the wick, and Mickey and Omar, spinning with beer and God and this church's long history, left, the white desert light from that yellow sun outside the building so harsh that both had to refit their sunglasses, making sure they rested on their noses and shaded their brown eyes comfortably before they got back in the car.

Mr. Crockett sat, as was his custom, sunning his eyes near the double doors of the Y, his white-tipped cane tapping against the glass. He was in a unique mood, first rocking himself back and forth anxiously as he leaned forward in his metal chair, then sliding his dulled wing-tip shoes on the linoleum, one foot forward, the other underneath. He didn't do this too long, and only one activity or the other, never the two at once. One time the movement of his left foot tangled up with his right and it caused him to moan, annoyed. That was the point when Mickey, before he was officially on duty behind the front desk for his shift, walked over to him and adjusted the unnecessary, indoors or out, overcoat Mr. Crockett was wearing—it was hanging limp off his shoulders and down his back and arms, about to fall off.

"So what's happening, Mr. Crockett?" Mickey also realigned the soft, beige fedora Mr. Crockett had let tilt too far down the side of his forehead. "You waiting for somebody? You're awful dressed up today."

"I'm . . . ," Mr. Crockett started, but the rest arrived unintelligible, a long drool. The subject, however, got him excited, and his feet shuffled as he raised his torso against the back of the chair.

"You sure you're okay, Mr. Crockett?" Mickey asked him again. Nobody'd seen Mr. Crockett behave this way before.

156

Mr. Crockett's mouth let out a long groaning sound, though broken coughs interrupted the steadier release of noise. Then he raised his head, too late, his eyes hopefully following the shadows of the two people who came through the front doors. Disappointed, he went back to rocking himself in the chair, swinging his shoulders and head, tapping the glass with his cane. Except now he began the moaning oh so quietly, and what might have been a tiny gurgle erupted, shaking something loose in his stomach. It was a nasty belch, and Mickey took it for his starting whistle.

Fred was feeling his vodka—which clearly felt good.

"How do you get that shit down?" Mickey asked. "Not *straight?*"

Fred grinned at him as he tried to slip his uncooperating arms into the sleeves of his Levi's jacket.

"What's with Mr. Crockett?" Mickey asked.

Fred shrugged his shoulders. "Long as he don't bother nobody. Long as he don't bother me."

"Something's going on."

"You see all kinds, see lots come and go," said Fred, content in his wisdom, his jacket finally fitted to his comfort. "That's all she wrote for this one. Look, you've got the mail today. It just got here and I'm just outta here."

"No shit," Mickey said, trying not to expose his own pleasure too much—not that Fred would have noticed. Mickey fondled the rubber-banded pile. "You have a good one, Fred. Keep having one."

Mr. Crockett's groaning had become obnoxious, and Oscar'd gone over to help—to force—him up to his room, but Mr. Crockett was resisting, fending him off, getting even louder. Fred not only didn't utter a word of encouragement to Oscar as he passed by, he didn't even acknowledge the scene. He pranced out the door.

Within a minute Mickey had skimmed through the stack looking for a letter for himself. But nothing.

Meanwhile, Oscar had decided to lift Mr. Crockett to his feet, and now was leading him toward the elevator. "You cannot wait all the day, Señor Crockett," Oscar tried to explain. "You have to go over your room right now."

"What's wrong with him, Oscar?" Mickey asked from behind the desk.

"No sé. Es que está loco, el viejito."

Suddenly Mr. Crockett moaned as Oscar escorted him— straight-armed him—into the elevator. The emotional sound wasn't clear—either laughter or a cry, it was not distinguishable.

Unfazed, distracted by his own confusions, Mickey began sorting the mail into two stacks, stopping twice because he had to punch the alphabet and number keys for patrons.

"This isn't right," said an average man dressed for the gym, one of the recipients of a transaction involving the money drawer.

"What isn't?" Mickey asked, not concentrating on this other work even yet.

"I gave you a twenty, and you gave me change for a ten."

"You must've given me a ten," Mickey told him, though he did not remember.

"I gave you a twenty," said the man, sure of himself.

"Are you positive?"

"Yes, I am."

"I don't know what to do," Mickey said primarily to himself. He considered asking Mrs. Schweitz, who was behind him at her desk. But he only considered it. "Well, okay, here's ten more. You seem pretty honest."

The man pocketed the money and, slightly peeved, went on his way.

Mickey worried for a split second, then returned to the mail sort. When he was done he took in the business envelopes to Mrs. Schweitz. She was consumed by her work, and he didn't say anything to her either.

Mickey began depositing the residents' mail in their proper slots. He couldn't restrain himself from short glances at the return addresses. He came upon one to Mr. Charles Towne. It was postmarked from New Orleans, and had clear tape on the flap. Money. Mickey knew it had to be money.

Right then Rosemary hugged him from behind, her soft breasts shoved into his back. Mickey jumped like he'd been scared by his first boo.

"Chingao! You about made my heart bust!"

"If *that*'s all it takes," Rosemary said, flirtatious.

"I didn't hear you coming," he told her, pronouncing each word well to compensate for his heart still not thumping rhythmically. "Wha'd you do, sneak up on me?"

"Not at all," she said. "It seems to me I could've been beating a drum and you wouldn't have noticed."

Mickey shook his head guiltily. He went back to directing the mail where it belonged more professionally, without an examination of each piece.

"So tomorrow night you come over," she said after she'd watched what he was doing for some seconds. She acted aroused by the prospect.

"Well," Mickey said. He was still reeling like he'd been caught at something. Right then she didn't even look so much better than nothing. He didn't even like women with huge breasts. And anyway there was something undesirable to him about eating at a mother's house. "I'm not sure I can."

"My mom said she'd take you after she's finished with

work,'' she said, cutting him off. ''She'll drive over. But I can drive back.'' She touched Mickey on the shoulder, like a secret signal he was supposed to understand. ''That would be good, wouldn't it?''

Mickey gave in. ''Yeah, why not?''

''All right, Momma?'' Rosemary asked loudly. ''Tomorrow?'' It was as though Rosemary assumed her mother had heard everything.

''Tomorrow what?'' Mrs. Schweitz asked.

''That Mickey comes over and you drive him there from here.''

''Oh.'' Mrs. Schweitz was hesitating—or she was so consumed by her work. ''If that's what you want.''

''See?'' said Rosemary.

Mickey, waiting calmly for Mrs. Schweitz to call it quits, stretched his legs out in the metal chair Mr. Crockett usually kept warm about this time of day. Oscar, leaning his starched and ironed gray work uniform into his usual spot for listening, listened and watched, at peace with his employment. Fred, working overtime, those hours taken away from Mickey, had slipped his glasses back into the fur-lined case clipped to the pocket of his favorite western shirt after an intricate transaction with a customer. Then he dug his rear into the metal stool behind the front desk, one boot heeled to a crossbar, the other rooted to the floor, staring off, sour or dulled, it was hard to tell—Mickey hadn't come around to buy him a whole or half-pint of vodka. Fred's brand of equanimity— Oscar's, too, for that matter—was especially impressive since Charles Towne, the band of his too small, logoless ball cap virtually shutting off blood into the skin around his skull, was taut with the conviction that someone was messing with his mail.

"I want my mail when it come," Charles demanded.

Charles's demands did not burden Fred with any unnecessary blasts of emotion.

"Don't know how come you ain't got it," Charles Towne repeated.

Mr. Fuller had been called to take charge of this outburst authoritatively and rounded the corner from his office. "What's the problem here?" he said with full military demeanor, just like the Sarge might in the same circumstances. He was wearing blue slacks and a gray jacket and a black tie, and the crisp tap of hard-polished shoes followed him behind the front desk and past the creaks of the swinging door and beside Fred.

"I want my mail when it come," Charles told him straight in the face.

"We've been through this before, Mr. Towne." Fuller's first impulse was stern.

"Don't matter."

"Charles," Mr. Fuller said sincerely, switching tactics, "we aren't keeping any of your mail. Honestly. We wouldn't have any reason to do such a thing."

"I got mail coming to me," Charles said, not willing to negotiate over another person's versions of the facts. "I know I got mail coming to me, and I want it."

"You looked carefully?" Mr. Fuller asked, turning to Fred. Fred nodded his head, unsympathetic, bored. "There simply is no mail here unless it's in your box now," Mr. Fuller affirmed to Charles.

"Ain't in my box." Charles's voice seemed to touch higher decibels, but it may have been the contrasting pall that had stricken the patrons of the cafeteria who'd gathered to listen at the perimeter, along with a few residents who'd exited the elevator, who joined some YMCA members on their way to or from the athletic facilities. There was, in other words, an audience gathering. Charles Towne, meanwhile, did not appear overly disturbed or upset, nor did he seem conscious, or self-conscious, about the people.

"Should be in my box but ain't," Charles espoused. "Should be in my hand. But ain't."

"Charles, what is it you want me to do?" Mr. Fuller asked him, frustrated.

"I want my mail when it *come.*"

Mr. Fuller was not too happy with the growing scene, by the folks gawking around, and his moods swayed this way and that, while his hands and feet fiddled and fidgeted. He pinched the bottom of his tie and tugged on it. "Charles, there is no mail for you today. That is all I can say." He shuffled his feet, squashed imaginary bugs. "Now . . . I want you . . . to please leave." Fuller's halting was for words of compromise—or something—but none came out. "Go to your room," he said, passing out the swinging door, suddenly righteous and firm. "I suggest you take a better look in your room. Maybe you forgot and you did get this mail."

Not a line in Charles's face lengthened. He didn't bend a digit.

"That's just as likely what happened," Mr. Fuller continued, speaking as much to Fred for backup and confirmation, trying as hard to maintain his composure as he did this reasoning. "You probably forgot, or maybe *you* lost it, not us. That's just as logical as what you're saying."

"I got mail coming to me, and I want it," Charles repeated, unmoved.

"Well, that's it!" Mr. Fuller yelled, his face flushed, his ears bright red. "That's enough of the show!" Fuller stormed past Charles and over to the people in front of the cafeteria, waving his palms. "Come on everybody, let's move on, everybody, please. You're not helping anything." Those near him backed up, and the timid ones even followed the instructions, but a few held their ground, scornful. So Mr. Fuller turned to Charles, as severe and cool as he could manage. "If you do not leave this subject alone immediately, *now,* I will have you physically escorted out. I will have you evicted."

Charles scowled dead at Mr. Fuller for what seemed minutes, his twisted eyebrows composing a familiar, for Charles, mix of nonsense and meaning, of the quizzical and the assured. Charles seldom went eye to eye like he did with Fuller, and never for so long.

"You gonna see, you gonna," he said. Charles had surrendered. He stepped away, circled a long route to the front doors and the air outside, stopping first next to Mickey, who was still in Mr. Crockett's chair. Charles edged up to him intimately, as one of his friends and confidants. "That's bullshit," he said, not screaming, but definitely not under his breath. "That's bullshit."

Mickey wished he didn't have to sit so near Mrs. Schweitz, but such was the nature of economy cars.

"Pretty wild today," he remarked.

Mrs. Schweitz didn't react as though she were knowledgeable on the topic—or like she was still consumed by her work.

"You know, with Charles Towne at the desk," he filled in.

"Oh, yes, that. Awful."

"Awful," Mickey said, parroting her for lack of other conversation. "I guess lots of people there come and go," he went on, trying on Fred's expression, also out of this same failure of material. "You must've seen lotsa stuff with people at the desk."

"Oh, well . . . " Mrs. Schweitz was changing lanes on I-10,

and she was concentrating on that. They were traveling east. "Well, yes, I suppose I have . . . I get nervous driving the freeway. I'm sorry."

"It's no problem," Mickey assured her, a little nervous himself about her driving on the interstate, since she was so uncomfortable. Though he didn't believe her. More likely it was him sitting there. He wondered when he caught on to this change in her attitude toward him—or was her attitude never what he'd thought? Because at first, he'd believed she was glad that he seemed to like her daughter, and that even before this she plain liked him.

"I put in a roast," Mrs. Schweitz said. "Well, Rosemary put it in the oven. I called her and told her to. And three-bean salad. Sweet potatoes." This was her turn to make conversation.

Mickey hated that bean salad and he hated sweet potatoes, and none of it sounded right together anyway. "Sounds delicious. I don't remember when I sat down at a table in someone's home and had a meal."

This didn't seem to spin music in Mrs. Schweitz's ears. "Roast beef. A rump roast."

"I love beef. The cow's what won the West, you know." So far, driving home with her was worse than he'd imagined. At least it was the same for her. "Put some chile on it and nobody could get it wrong." Clearly the wrong thing to say. "Did you ever see that reverend, the Reverend Miller the Third, that guy?" he said, attempting to change material quick. "He was crazed about the mail too. Makes you wonder. Makes you wonder about the importance of the mail to some people."

Mrs. Schweitz nervously patted her hair-sprayed bouffant like she'd find something she'd lost. "Oh, well, the people who live there, they sometimes receive checks or cash. Or they're lonely and they open mail from their children or relatives. People need those things. Sometimes I think getting mail is the only hope some of them still have. It may be their last contact with a world that had to have been better for them than the one they're living at the YMCA, all alone in those rooms.''

Mickey allowed that to digest. ''That's a real nice thing you said there,'' he told her. ''Real sensitive and intelligent. I live there, you know. And what you say is the absolute truth.''

His reaction caught Mrs. Schweitz unprepared. It flattered her, which did good for both of them. She was encouraged. ''People who live there, most of them are decent and good. I don't think anyone would live there if they didn't have to, and the elderly ones are there because they are strong enough to take care of themselves and not be in homes.''

''Then there's guys like me, and Butch, and John Hooper . . .'' Mickey caught himself making a list. ''Though I'm not going to be there much longer,'' he explained with the typical resident's shame. ''I'm trying hard to get out. Been there way longer than I ever expected.''

''Well, I hope . . .'' She couldn't find the end of the sentence, and they drove in silence until it was given up as lost.

''So did you ever see that Reverend Miller?''

''No. Unless he's the one that Joe, Mr. Fuller, evicted not so long ago.''

''I think so,'' he said. ''I'm not sure, but I think.''

''He was the one who kicked the cigarette machine too.''

''That's the reverend. He did that during my shift.''

''I never saw him, and I don't know what he looks like. But if it's the same person, he's made threatening phone calls and the police were contacted.''

''Really? Whadaya mean?''

"Death threats."

"No lie?"

"That's what I was told. We've had these problems about the mail before."

Mickey became uncomfortable again. "You mean it *has* been missing?"

"Personally, I don't think so. I think these people want it to be. Then their imagination takes over."

Mickey was impressed again. "Like Charles Towne."

"Mr. Fuller has been hearing his complaints about mail since he moved in. I don't mean to sound bigoted, but black people always cause trouble. I don't know why that is."

"Charles has a couple problems, but he's good people," Mickey said in his defense. "And maybe his mail got lost at the post office or something. Who knows?"

Mrs. Schweitz was steering toward the off-ramp, which was a great idea for both of them. "We're almost home now," she said.

"I really appreciate you letting me come over."

Mrs. Schweitz looked the opposite direction of Mickey's face. "I spoil her. I couldn't stop her from asking you." Now she looked straight at him. "She's never had a boyfriend before."

"Never had a boyfriend? I thought, like, wasn't there a GI?"

Mrs. Schweitz shook her head. "Nobody. Look, I'm going to tell you something. You better not do anything, you understand? You better not hurt her. Nothing personal now, but if I had any say in it—I don't mean to offend you—but I can't believe my daughter has a crush on a resident, someone like you. I don't mean to offend you, but I don't like it very much."

Mickey looked straight ahead.

* * *

Mickey, his jaw limp with misery, sat at the head of the maple table. Devout, Rosemary was practicing at wife. A ruffly apron on, pot holders gloving each hand, she had scurried in and out of the kitchen to arrange the table setting most decorously, and now, from the dinner table, gracious, passing around the unglazed ceramic Mexican bowls and glazed china plates to him first and foremost, demanding that he load up his plate. She ate her own moderate helping delicately, cutting the overcooked meat into tiny bites, suggesting that she'd never overeaten her entire life. From her pillowed chair, Mrs. Schweitz slouched downward into her meal, frowning, though it showed up as a tilted smile on her face. Maybe because of this atmosphere, and since Mickey couldn't appreciate the food—no chile to help it out—Mickey had asked— and knew to pretend otherwise, or maybe because it was and had been true about her all along, what Omar said, tonight he saw her too well, not through Oscar's eyes. Reality, Mickey too often realized in sorrow, sucked the fun out of life.

As the women cleared the table, Mickey was directed to the room where the furniture went unused, its wood veneers spray polished, the foam stuffing cushions in the flowery couch sets, still spongy with newness, tugged into neater squares, the glass on the high school photographs of Rosemary washed and shined. The thick synthetic no-stick carpet glittered with bristly treated fibers and had just been vacuumed, and un-dog-eared magazines on the table, on Southern living and lifestyle, were tiered for display as in the floor room of a department store.

Mickey, a little disappointed, even if he was full, concentrated on his sorry condition: He didn't have any car, he didn't have any better woman than this big old monster girl with big old breasts, he didn't have any money, he barely had what went as a job, and he still had hours to go before he would, or could, return to, of all places, his room 412 of the YMCA.

Rosemary came and plopped next to him, cheerful. "Hi."
She tried to be as close to him as she could without contact.
"Good dinner," Mickey exaggerated. "Thanks for having me
over." He was sitting as far forward at the edge of the couch as
possible. He didn't attempt to wrap his arm around her, even
though he knew she expected it.

"I bet you could come over just about anytime."

"I doubt it," Mickey snickered.

"Why do you say that?"

"Your mom." He was bringing this up not to straighten
things out so he'd be invited again, but precisely for the opposite
effect.

"Did she say something to you?" asked Rosemary, concerned.

"It's that she didn't say anything."

Rosemary got upset.

"I'm sorry," he assured her. "I don't mean to start anything.
I should shut up."

"Well, I feel bad now. I want you to like it here." She
pondered. "Sit back." Now she made the move, scooting her
body against him, her head weakening to his shoulder.

Soon she'd pushed him so that all of him, shoulders and
everything, were ensconced in the couch, and she cuddled
sweetly. It continued to grow on Mickey what this was conjuring
up in her romantic mind, which was not at all the conception he
had in his own.

"Really, I'm sorry," he told her. "I'm probably being over-
sensitive or something. And I'm sure your mom's just tired from
work."

Rosemary was relieved.

"You're the first boy to eat with us. Maybe it's that."

That was precisely what Mickey was afraid of. "So what about that other guy, your boyfriend from Fort Bliss?"

"Are you kidding?"

"No, huh. So why've you been going out with him then?"

Rosemary shrugged her shoulders.

"Wouldn't he be jealous if he knew I was here right now?"

"Stop it," she said.

"I don't want to get in the way of things for you guys."

"Stop it. You know it's nothing serious between him and me."

"You're telling me." He considered going after it, but decided to stay dumb. "Whatever you say. But I better be careful. He's big and tough, right?"

"I'm sorry we have to be in here," Rosemary said, changing the subject. "My mom thinks it's better in here than in the TV room. There's more light in here, so it's safer or something. To her."

Mickey started thinking about Jake and Consuela. Consuela had big breasts too, and he had an unmistakable image of how lovely they were. Consuela was beautiful. Rosemary was not beautiful. That was the honest to God truth, and truth was an important variable. She probably did not have breasts as beautiful as Consuela either. But he decided that, well, it maybe was better to err on the side of action, not inaction. Especially since no one else would have to know. So Mickey reached into her blouse moments after he began kissing her.

"No!" she said, pushing his hand off.

"How come?"

"You know I like you, but I'm not easy."

Mickey didn't joke.

"Besides," she said, "my mom might come in." She snuggled up forgivingly. "I do like you," she repeated, "and I still have to take you back."

Mickey didn't tell Rosemary how happy that made him. "I'm the kinda guy you shouldn't like too much," he told her, paraphrasing a speech Jake made to Consuela, though in his case it was after he'd made love to her and her incredibly flawless body. Mickey's intention might have been less noble or heroic, but he thought it better to not seem that way. "I got too much wild blood. I can't be tied to any one woman."

"Maybe the right one," Rosemary said. She angled her breasts into his shoulder and triceps.

"Not possible," Mickey assured her. He told her a variation of the story about the cocktail waitress in Albuquerque, this one having a moral about him leaving her because he had to, along the same lines Jake gave Consuela. "That's the kind of man I am," he stated. "It's the pleasure of this minute. *Now.* If not now, then not never."

"It's getting late," Rosemary said. Mickey had talked a while. "I'll take you back." Rosemary disappeared from the room and returned with Mrs. Schweitz.

"Come back again," Mrs. Schweitz said insincerely and sour.

"Sure," Mickey said heartily. "Dinner was real good. Thanks a lot."

"You don't take too long," Mrs. Schweitz warned Rosemary, "and drive carefully. I mean it," she said, meaning the first half of the command.

Rosemary nodded her head, innocent, as they went out the front door.

"We'll see you at work!" Mickey waved from under the darkness at Mrs. Schweitz. They drove in the direction of the Y, but not on the interstate. Neither said too much. They passed by a few minimarts.

"Let's stop a few minutes," Mickey said. "I'll buy beer." It was all he could afford.

"If you had a car," she reproached him, "we could go out, and then I could really drink with you for a while." She stopped at a brightly lit, plastic façade. "Buy peanuts. Buy me some candy with peanuts."

Mickey brought back the candy bar and a quart of beer. He had less than a quarter. It was all he had left in the world until he got paid.

The engine off, they could hear taps playing from the fort, a breeze guiding the bugle toward them.

"There's your boyfriend," Mickey said. He downed more than her.

"There's nothing going on between us," she said, chewing. "How come you keep saying that?"

"He might come after me. You already told me how jealous he was."

"Well, you're not afraid of him, are you?"

"Should I be?"

"Maybe if I told him. You better be nice to me."

"If you're nice to me, I'll be nice to you." Mickey could not believe how unattractive Rosemary was tonight, and still he kissed her, and she let him. Then he reached at her breasts, and she let him. He reached under her blouse, and she let him. He reached behind and unhooked her brassiere and they burst free, soft and huge. Mickey found it nice to feel warm breasts—it had been so long. Even if they weren't Consuela's breasts. Or Ema's. Ema's. But these were Rosemary's breasts. And, in the throes of caressing them, he reminded himself that he would like them more as time passed, when he wasn't touching them. He would remember them more affectionately, through memory, than he did now, in fact, through touch. They were this Rosemary's breasts, and maybe he would think of them, of her, like he did that girl back then who loved him so much, who he loved so much in his mind these years later. This time he wouldn't have to regret missing the opportunity. He'd remember Rosemary and her breasts romantically when he was lonely again.

He reached between her legs, and she let him until she stopped him. She pushed his hand away. Then she started the car. "We have to move away from this light." She shifted into reverse, her body half-spun toward the back window. "My mom will make it awful for both of us," she said as an aside, an afterthought.

"Both of us?"

"She can have you fired, you know."

"You mean through Big Ears? Quelá, that never crossed my mind."

Nonetheless, Rosemary fit the car into a parking slot by an unlit side of the building.

"Your mom tell you about work today?" Mickey asked. "About the scene with this guy named Charles Towne?"

She shook her head.

"The guy thinks someone's hiding his mail, taking it. Mr. Fuller threatened him with the police."

"Maybe somebody is," she said.

"Whadaya mean?"

"Maybe someone is ripping off his mail."

Mickey didn't want to play this.

"You've seen the mail the residents get there. I saw you the other day. I've done that too. Me and Mária have. You know what I mean."

"I didn't do shit! What're you talking about?"

"When sometimes you can tell there's an interesting letter inside an envelope, or there's money."

"You mean *you've* taken it?"

"I'd never take anything of yours even if I did take someone else's," she promised. "And I never said I did. Don't get so upset."

"Jesus," Mickey said.

"I didn't say I did it, you know. I'm just kidding you."

Mickey gripped the door handle.

"I was only teasing," she said, moving her hips into his bucket seat. "I was teasing you because you're so sensitive about it."

Mickey didn't pop the door latch.

Rosemary leaned more of herself into him still, and began kissing him apologetically. Mickey let her. "I like you," she said. "I want you to like me."

Mickey was hiding out in El Paso. Mickey was having something dizzying like a premonition, fragments of one, and he didn't know what about it was true, what was made up. This was evidence that something bad was bound to happen, and it would be his fault. The letter that was supposed to come to him, the money, it wasn't going to, it never was. Or it was the letter he was looking at, the one he'd been caught looking at, with the tape, to Charles Towne. It was a confusing story, and then Rosemary grabbed between his legs and it felt so good and it kept feeling so good that he rubbed between her legs and her breasts.

"The team's been playing super, Coach."

"Thanks. I do think we're playing real good."

"You're gonna have to go up against those other guys next. How do you prepare for a game as important as that?"

"I don't have to do much really. We all know what it means. My job is to keep everything in perspective."

"And to win."

"That too."

"You think you can beat them?"

"I know we can. We will."

"What happens if you lose?"

"We won't."

"But if you do? What would you say?"

"That won't happen."

"If it did, though. Honestly."

"Honestly?"

"Yes."

"Not my job to talk about that."

"It happens, right? Come on."

"Well, I'd say how the loss didn't count. That it didn't matter. Concentrate on the next game, the next team, that that wasn't the real game."

Step out. Start over. That's not the game. That's not how it works. Ball back and forth. Win. Almost lose, but win. Only wins. The guy has the ball. It's his to win or lose. It's his. Not about losing.

Mickey hadn't played ping-pong for a couple of weeks. Charles Towne tuned his paddle almost every day, and was winning with it—he was undefeated in Mickey's absence. Still, Charles was so private about his ping-pong skills and aspirations that he'd never brought it up once in Mickey's presence, even as he stood almost next to him—eyes cocked, mouth a touch opened—observing Mickey push the free weights just as he used to before he'd been kicked off the Universal machine.

"Are you sure he wants to play with me?" Mickey asked Butch one night. "He's gotten lots of chances to say something to me and he hasn't."

"It's what he tells everybody," said Butch. "He says he want to beat you. Que va a ganar if you play him horita."

A challenge, which did sound exciting. The fans in Mickey's mental coliseum hushed with the anticipation of a championship match.

"He was pretty upset that last time," Mickey said. "No recuerdes?"

Butch nodded, raising his eyebrows. "That booshit," he joked in his whisper.

"I dunno, man," Mickey worried. "Charles is good people."

"What's the big deal?" said Omar. "It's fucking ping-pong."

Even the Sarge, who cared so much about his games but never a little about ping-pong, who scoffed at going in that room with, as he put it, those unemployables, was drawn to this. "Afraid you'll lose?" he asked Mickey.

Mickey resisted saying something about the only time the Sarge beat anything. "I'm afraid he'll lose," he said. "I'm afraid it'll fuck him up."

"Secret agents can't lose," Omar cracked. "Even when it looks like they lost, they might've won."

Butch's body shook with what went as laughter for him. The Sarge took no position on the joke.

Mickey entered the ping-pong room.

"Hey Charles!" Mickey called out, laying both hands on the big table. "I hear you're looking for a showdown." He'd picked up a gritty-faced paddle and swatted the air.

Charles tensed up.

"Wanna play?" Mickey asked. Though he couldn't make light of it with Charles, he refused to be too serious.

Charles approached an end of the ping-pong table and tapped a ball toward Mickey.

"I guess this means que sí," Mickey said, hitting it back.

"You say when you warmed up," Charles finally spoke out. "Get two outta three games."

They batted it back and forth a few times, and Mickey told him he was and Charles should serve. Charles wanted to do it the right way, by volleying three times first. Mickey lost. Charles led 4–1 after his opening serve, then 7–3, then 11–4, then 13–7, then 16–9, and so on until the first game was his, 21–13.

"Well, Charles, guess I'm gonna have to play a lot tougher if I'm gonna beat you."

Charles concentrated, his brain restraining screams of anxiety—but they were in his eyes, which were opened so wide they had to hurt, they were on his forehead, taut lines pulled from either side of his temple.

Mickey wanted the next game. It was important to him to prove that he could win whenever he decided, at his will. It would be his own personal evidence and then, if he had to, he could lose the next game and thereby the match, knowing it was only a choice he'd made. His strategy was to settle back, return the ball, take advantage of Charles when he played an easy one, then strike even harder when Charles's confidence faltered. And Mickey took every service, his own and Charles's, by at least 3–2.

Mickey broke away to drink some water. He was about to ask the Sarge advice—because the Sarge was someone who found these contests so significant—about the meaning of winning or losing. A practical question of philosophy that the Sarge would be glad to answer. It was why he was attending, to see, to interpret for himself. More than visualizing the psychology of victory or defeat, the Sarge was there to see the real human response to it.

Mickey didn't like or trust the Sarge, he wasn't anyone

who'd give him advice. Get a job, he'd say. He was right, that's what Mickey needed. But was the Sarge a sex weirdo? How that related, Mickey wasn't sure. Some power deal. Why was he here? Because the Sarge, Mickey'd say, kept getting his butt beat, and he came to see Mickey lose. The Sarge was sick and tired of and outright disgusted with Mickey winning. The Sarge was figuring that Mickey would finally lose, since his winning wasn't—according to the Sarge's well-developed instincts—based on talent or skill or, most of all, discipline, that it had to end.

The Sarge wanted to be there to see him lose. If Mickey lost to Charles, he could lose to the Sarge. The Sarge would be inspired, and the Sarge could win, then the Sarge could gloat . . .

So many things wrong with Mickey. His thinking was not too clear. He couldn't keep up with all the confusions and disconnections.

Mickey played without conscience. Mickey didn't *just* win either, he broke and shattered Charles Towne in the third game.

Charles shook his head slowly and mumbled as he paced the ping-pong room, searching, it seemed once he located it, the door out. Some of the guys, who'd played him many times the past days, residents recent and not so, razzed him about getting his payback. But nobody really cared if this guy named Charles Towne or this one called Mickey Acuña won or lost. Charles, however, didn't know that, or if he did, it didn't matter anyway, because he didn't lose only the match. He left the ping-pong room defeated, humiliated—he was a child who didn't make the team and whose life had changed because of it.

"Charles!" Mickey yelled, running to the elevator. "I'm sorry." Words at the absolute limit of Mickey's vocabulary.

But Charles wasn't mad at Mickey, though maybe only because Charles was too overcome by an exaggerated swirl of self-obsessed emotion—his vision broken like glass, his foggy stare seeking an unseeable distance—and there wasn't any space available for being mad at someone else.

V

It wasn't entirely Mickey. It was also the night. Or the moon, or
the wind, or the dark. Or maybe the fates, those juices no one
knows and never will. But not, Mickey was sure, meaningless
chance—that wouldn't explain who these guys were, taking up
lobby space, draping themselves over the desk, bored. Probably it
did have to do with the ping-pong match between Mickey and
Charles the night before—nobody felt like playing after all that
excitement. So instead they were clumped up with nowhere else
to go, near Mickey and the front desk. Mickey could have told
them they couldn't be there, which is what he was supposed to do,
but he didn't see that as his duty, and he couldn't say anything, this
was definitely not his style. Besides, he felt the same unmeaningful
urge for a break in the routine too. Which was why he brought out
the TV. A small black-and-white from the office, hidden in the
closet, doing nothing in a back corner but being next to a couple
of cardboard boxes, soaking up the same dust. Mickey positioned
the TV on the far edge of the formica counter as the best possible
view for everyone and himself, then plugged it in. It worked fine
enough and he spun the dial until he tuned in a boxing match, a

welterweight fight televised on a station from Mexico City. And so the guys closed in on the desk, content, stimulated even. There were five men at first, then seven, then maybe ten residents shoving against and around the front desk. All of them genuinely liked Mickey right then, thought he was a top of the line dude, one of them, the first among equals. They smoked cigarettes and broke out some beers—kept them in the brown sacks, since they knew the rules and didn't want to get Mickey in trouble.

Now that everybody's attention had been pleasantly diverted, Mickey used his free time to go to the mailboxes. And there it was: Directly below Charles's box was the letter with the New Orleans return address, the one with the tape over the back flap. It would be easy to explain the mix-up. Rosemary had surprised him. And, he'd say and insist, the implication not being worthy of defense, he did not put it there then, he *found* it there. He thought maybe he should leave it and show Fred or Mrs. Schweitz first, but then he wanted more that Charles know right away.

"Oiga, Butch. Do me a favor. Traígame la cabeza del señor Charles. I got a hot news flash for him." Mickey was ecstatic with relief.

Butch didn't hesitate to take the elevator trip. He wasn't into boxing. Omar wasn't watching the fight either. He elbowed the counter at an opposite corner like someone who wanted to be alone at the bar, sullen, irritable, looking for trouble.

"I found the mail he was worrying about," Mickey told him. "It was there all along. Just that nobody saw it."

Omar wasn't interested in other people's problems. He lifted his own brown bag. It was a thin flask of sweet Mexican brandy.

"Take a pill, man," Mickey told him. "You need one."

At least that provoked a grin. "You're all right, cuñado. I'm gonna remember you in my will."

"Me and Uncle Sam." Mickey felt better too.

"Let's get the fuck outta here," Omar said. "Go get fucked up somewheres."

There were two men outside, leering inside, one of them nosing his face into the glass. Mickey knew the double doors ought to be unlocked, but went over to check in case. One side was, the other wasn't. The two men there backed off into the darkness, nervous, like they'd been doing something they shouldn't. Mickey was just about to say something to them when he saw Blind Jimmy struggling to walk with a heavy box strapped on his shoulder and under an arm, the all-white cane occupying the other side. Mickey cut off his curiosity about the two men and jogged over to Jimmy.

"You got a load there! You coming to the Y?"

"Yes I am," Jimmy said, disoriented and unsure who was talking to him, what it meant that he was being spoken to.

"I'll help you out." Mickey grabbed the weight off Blind Jimmy's back. "It's all right," he said, sensing Jimmy's worry. "I work there. Hey, this is an accordion, ain't it?"

"Yes. Yes it is." Jimmy's eyes spun.

"And you can play it?" Mickey rested a hand on Blind Jimmy's shoulder to guide him along, though Jimmy still tapped for a feel of the sidewalk as they approached the doors of the Y.

"Yes. I do." He was proud.

"I never knew anyone who could play one before. That's pretty all right, man."

Jimmy was complimented. "I've played it since I was very young," he bragged.

"That is *too cool,*" Mickey said, pulling open the unlocked half of the double door.

The two other men, still standing away from the light, came in behind them.

"Well, thank you." Jimmy was so unaccustomed to praise his face had blushed, the veiny whites of his eyes rolling around youthfully, happy. The volume of the fight on the tube wasn't nearly as high as the men around it. They buzzed and hooted like a real crowd high above ringside.

"Don't mind the guys here. It's just a fight, a boxing match on the tube. So you need a room?"

Jimmy was fascinated. "Thank you."

Mickey unhooked a room key from the rack and helped him fill out the registration card. "It's on the house but don't tell on me. Maybe you could play that thing for us sometime. You think?"

"Oh yes." Now Jimmy was honored.

Mickey put the key in Jimmy's palm and told him it was room 414. "You're right next to me now," he said, "so you better not party later than I do."

A knockdown, an eight count. The Y crowd turned more boisterous than the one in the television. Blind Jimmy stood there expectant, a smile on his lips, his ears wide open, holding the key like he was letting it air out.

"If you gimme a second, I'll find someone to take you upstairs," Mickey said. He briefly acknowledged that Jimmy had no luggage, nothing but the accordion, and he might have talked about that if those other two men—one of them—hadn't asserted their presence at the front desk.

"Are rooms available?" the burly, dark-haired one asked with a strong New York accent. He'd been talking friendly to Omar, and Mickey assumed they knew each other. His beard was so heavy he had to use a razor twice a day to keep the pockmarks on his face visible. The clean shave didn't make him look wholesome.

"They are," Mickey began. He stopped himself from doing Fred's lines. "Only got one left with a toilet in it. One man to one room, though."

He walked far off to the side and against the wall and near the cigarette machine the Reverend Miller had dented, where his friend hunched, hiding, like he was afraid to be looked at. He was lean, with long tan hair tucked behind his ears and under a blue beret. He seemed overly afraid to stand straight, his head turtled into his neck, like he preferred being out from under the artificial light and in the natural darkness. He never looked up. He never moved. The two of them conferenced privately.

"We'll take that one luxury suite and one other," the accent announced as it returned.

Mickey slid two registration forms onto the counter. "Planning to stay long?"

"I think just for the night," he said. He used a money clip.

"So you're not even gonna spend one night out in the Wild West?" Omar asked him. "How could they let that happen, cuñado?" he asked Mickey. He stared at one and then the other. "They look like pretty tough hombres to me."

This huskier guy was named Harry something—Mickey couldn't make out a last name on the registration card. As to his address he made it clear: USA. Mickey didn't contest the specifics like Fred complained he was supposed to, though he almost decided to get at least something in writing from the beret—Mickey didn't like the looks of that guy.

A howl flew up because the fight came to an end. A technical knockout. The guys around the TV were calling the ruling in different directions, arguing about who really got the best in and who took the worst. Not thinking, his attention on several subjects at once, Mickey plucked off two more keys and handed them to this Harry. Another night, other circumstances, he might have felt more remorse than he did for giving this Harry these keys so easily after he'd paid for them.

"I know bars with *long-legged* mommies," Omar used as bait, "and my compa here, he lets us bring them up to our room whenever we want. Ain't that right, cuñado?"

Mickey didn't say. Now he had his eye on the beret. What was it with that dude? A thief? A drug addict? Something going on with him. He was too jumpy, too restless, too secretive.

Harry, whatever his last name, talked and laughed with Omar—he even took a hit off of Omar's brandy. "Well, it sounds fucking-A good to me," he said. He nodded toward the cigarette machine. "My partner, I think he's feeling too tired and needs to get his beauty sleep."

"Well, then, we'll make it party time without that punk!" Omar said, transcending his sorry mood. "You get rid of that sorry friend of yours and make your colita ready, ese!"

Mickey was about to make some polite noise about the beret when Blind Jimmy, who Mickey'd forgotten once this other business was taken on, began working the keys of the accordion. A polka style, like a regular on Lawrence Welk.

"We'll find us some *very* long-legged mamitas," Omar was saying as though nothing else was happening in the room. "And we can fucking-A do that, can't we, cuñado? We'll fucking-A the town." Omar was swallowing bigger and bigger gulps of brandy. "We'll go to the Saloon," he said, taking himself more seriously. "We'll listen to music. We'll dance. You wanna hear cowboy music, ain't that right? That's a cowboy bar, and that's where you wanna go. Right?"

Harry was occupied by the whole show—Blind Jimmy made hoops of sound, danced with thick petticoats and bolo ties—and not just Omar. "Sure," he said, distracted.

And then Butch appeared at the desk and Mickey couldn't make out a word. He asked again and still couldn't hear.

And then Charles was there. The two guys from the USA had entered the elevator as he'd exited.

"Check your mailbox," Mickey told him.

Charles lumbered over to it, oblivious to the accordion and the guys around the television. Mickey ran around to the other side of the glass windowed case. Charles opened the little mailbox and saw Mickey's face and nothing between.

"Look below, Charles," Mickey told him. "In the box directly below."

Charles gradually made logic of what Mickey'd said, and his eyes and head caught up.

"See that?" Mickey said, pointing, then he reached in for the envelope. He glided it out the lower slot and into the upper one like a Christmas present, and Charles, catching on a second or a few after, pulled it out from his side of the wall.

Mickey hurried around the front desk. The accordion stretched and shrank against Jimmy's chest, his pale fingers having perfect sight for its keyboard, and then he even began to sing, wobbling on his feet, back and forth, side to side, like a drunk, his voice pitched high not to just sound like a girl, but a baby girl.

Charles didn't want to open the letter, and his face was still mostly blank.

"That mail was there all along," Mickey interpreted it for him. "You see, Charles?"

"Ain't it," Charles said.

Mickey didn't believe Charles understood. "Open it, Charles. It's it, it's gotta be it."

"Don't got to. It ain't it."

And then the man in the suit who'd come the other time for Jimmy shoved through the open half of the double door. He pounded right up to Jimmy, impolitely this time, and put an end to the music.

Charles did not seem to intuit any shift in atmosphere, though it was as subtle as a flushing toilet.

"He's going to help me to get my operation," Jimmy told everybody. "The first thing I want are some cute shoes."

The man in the suit glowered at Mickey, his jaws quivering. He was a gentleman, so this was the furthest physical reach of his anger. "He shouldn't be here. We try very hard to take care of him. Why would you encourage him?"

"I didn't know," Mickey said. "I'm just the desk clerk, and he wanted a room."

The man in the suit was not understanding. "He lives right around the corner! Everyone knows that!" He picked up Blind Jimmy's white cane and handed it to him, grunted as he loaded the accordion box onto his shoulder, then led Blind Jimmy to the front doors and out.

The party over, the guys began separating, pairing off to find a liquor store, or, alone, calling it a day.

"But the night is young," Omar told Mickey, enunciating his syllables, "and you're off in less than an hour. We gonna be *bad* boys tonight."

"That's got to be the mail," Mickey told Charles again.

Charles shook his head. He was without a doubt.

"I do need to get the fuck outta here," Mickey replied. "But I ain't got a dime."

"Don't know how you gonna do without me around, cuñado," Omar said. He finished off the brandy and threw the empty bottle into the trash can behind the desk.

* * *

Omar had snuggled into a cheap, broad-lapeled white suit with matching vest, was straightening the collar of a black shirt and centering a white tie. The slacks had a slight bell bottom to them, while at the other end, his stepping-out hat was spiffed up by a short, fluffy feather.

"You got yourself a fine hat there, compa," Mickey said, "but I'm not sure about that feather you pulled from your pillow." Mickey didn't tell him how he'd be the envy of all the other guys on a dance floor dressed like hip insurance salesmen.

"You think this tie looks better than the other one?" Omar asked.

To Mickey they were twins. "The one you got on."

"We gotta look like we got some style." As always, his voice made it sound like he was in fact kidding, it just didn't make sense that he was. "So get your act ready," Omar told Mickey. "Even our secret agent man's putting on one of my new shirts."

"Charles? He's going?" Charles had never been anywhere with them before.

"Damn straight. It's a party, cuñado!" Omar knotted his tie in the mirror one more time, balanced his hat once more, and turned. "Do I look like a *vato* or not?"

Mickey nodded graciously.

"So you gonna wear something, or you gonna go like that?" Mickey had on dirty Levi's and the long-sleeve white shirt he'd been wearing for lots of days.

"Maybe not. I'd feel like trail dust you guys'll be kicking up."

"I got something here you could wear." Omar threw him a shiny, patterned polyester shirt—fake silk—that was the disco fashion rage in Juárez. "I bought a couple at the same time I did this suit."

"It won't fit me," Mickey said, "and I wouldn't want to mess up one of your new shirts."

"Well, you gotta come anyways, cuñado, because I already gave my car to Butch, and we're celebrating. And you gotta help us catch *long-legged* women. You know I'm counting on you, 'cuz I *know* how *good* you are with them."

Mickey didn't care for his tone. "Did I tell you about Rosemary?" Mickey hadn't mentioned it yet because he wasn't exactly proud of himself. He also didn't like being jealous about that car fucking Omar didn't give *him*.

"Don't be talking so foulmouthed," Omar moaned. "Tonight we're gonna get us some ladies who gotta be looking *good.*"

"Serious, man. I went over to her house the other night."

Omar pretended he couldn't hear.

Mickey couldn't be sure if he didn't believe him, or did and was too disgusted. "She's not that bad. She's real nice. Honest."

"Let's go," Omar said, excited. "Harry is waiting downstairs with Butch and Mr. Charleston, who *as you know* is from New Orleans." He was feeling little pain.

"It's not that I love her or some stupid shit like that." Mickey couldn't let him get away with the last word. "She's the one that wants me. But then I'm not the kinda guy who'd wanna hurt her feelings either. Besides, she feels better than nothing." He was trying to hint but be obvious too.

Omar ignored it for several seconds, but when he spoke, his voice got deeper, and sober. "You gotta stop it, cuñado. It's gonna fuck your brains up." He shook two Dilaudids from an aspirin jar. He tested a can of soda, but it was empty. He pocketed the pills for later.

Mickey'd considered several possible defenses against Omar

about Rosemary—nobody was perfect, not him, not her, not Omar—but not being believed about her would've never occurred to him.

"I'm not bullshitting you. Fuck, I don't wanna hear your shit no more. Butch told me, you know."

Omar laughed his way out of it. "Qué pues, hombre? I meant you shouldn't make puñeta with the Sarge no more." He cackled over his own humor. "Can't you take no joke?"

Mickey nodded.

Omar was talking loud to Harry so that he could be heard above the taped music coming from the nightclub speakers. Though he would have been heard well anyway. Harry didn't seem to mind their table being the locus of narrow glares radiating in on them from all sides. "Butch took that bottle," he said, "y entonces, *poom!,* un chingazo across the head and the vato went down, like for good night."

"And then what did you do?" Harry asked, amused and impressed.

"We got the fuck outta there de volada, como fast!"

Harry laughed from his gut. "The Wild West, huh?" he said, showing off his sophisticated, big-city memory.

"Andale! The Wild West! Verdad, cuñado?" Omar was acknowledging that this line came from Mickey.

Out of all the times Mickey'd heard the story, never once was he mentioned in it, not once was there any description of him dropping Fernie's brother Louie. It was as though that part never happened. Which made him think: It did happen. So why did he have to tell himself that it *really* did? Why were they fucking with him?

"The Wild West," Omar went on. "Good guys and bad guys, Consuelo, and Consuela, and Jake. Qué no?"

Butch laughed, in his manner, too.

Mickey did believe it was the Wild West, good guys and bad guys, Consuelas and Jakes. Here it was, he'd say, blustering into this Harry, with the New York accent, from the USA.

"So tell about Rosemary," Omar remembered. "This guy," he told Harry, "he can tell the stories. Yeah, he's got the stories he can tell."

Mickey caught Omar's insider glance—like an elbow, or a wink—at Butch. And Butch's smirk meant he was conspiring with Omar. Mickey couldn't believe he'd been so wrong about Butch, or if Butch hadn't believed him all along either.

"So go on," Omar prodded him.

Mickey shook his head. Not to say no but to let it be clear he was very pissed off.

"Then tell about that other bullshit," Omar shoved on, pushing it. "That outlaw shit. How you're kinda hiding out, *hole-ing* up, waiting around the Y because you got to." Omar's drunken speech, slurring its mock sincerity, had raised Mickey's intelligence. He began to reason very precisely about how he could kick Omar's fat butt, about where, precisely, his nose would crack, about which teeth, exactly, would break off easiest. Besides his size advantage, Mickey had been working out every day, had missed only that one day since he'd been there, and at this moment he felt it was by design, not accident. Intentional.

"He's being shy," Omar continued. "He told us how some bad news might be coming down soon if things don't happen like he was promised. He don't know what, but . . . poes, come on, you tell 'em, cuñado."

Harry, not without the usual instincts, quit looking at either of these guys, and quit smiling.

Right then Mickey decided it'd only be a few more nights. He would hit the road, give up.

"Better yet," Omar said, his slur turning into a slobber, "ask this other dude here about his job. Tell him, Charles."

Charles was wearing one of Omar's new polyester shirts. It was a size too small in the shoulders, an inch or even two too short in the arm length. He still had on the same baggy pants he always had on, and suspenders, and the cap still covered his head. He was drinking beer, was supposed to be, he just spent more time staring at the bottle it came in.

"He's a secret agent," Omar confided.

Uncertain, Harry wasn't sure what the appropriate response was.

"For reals," Omar went on. "Tell him."

Mickey saw that Charles wasn't right. He'd been getting worse, almost by the hour, since that ping-pong game. "Leave 'em alone," he warned Omar.

"He don't mind saying. Watch." Omar steadied his voice. "You're a secret agent, ain't that right, Charles?"

Charles both shook and nodded his head, slowly, without his eyes wandering off the label of the beer bottle.

"Fucking leave him alone *now*," Mickey told Omar again. "You're a fucking asshole, and he won't fuck with you, but I *will*."

"You worry too much, cuñado. He don't mind, does he, Butch?"

Butch was rubbing the fuzz on his head, keeping his opinion quiet.

"I wanna be," Charles relented, somewhere between proud and pathetic. "I'm not one yet."

"You see!" said Omar, triumphant. "That's all right!" Omar slugged Charles in the shoulder, then tried to lean over to give him a sloppy hug.

"Leave him alone, Omar," Mickey threatened. He stood up and pushed Omar back into his chair. "You fucking asshole." Mickey didn't know whose side Butch was on. Though he didn't care, he wanted to know now. For all the time they'd spent together, he knew next to nothing about Butch. But since Omar had given him a car, he'd reasoned, maybe that was all it took.

"Should we go?" Harry asked Mickey. "Is that better?" Harry had no difficulty understanding that they were in a situation. And they were bringing on a lot more attention than before, especially from the big fellows at the door.

"Let's hear some music first," Mickey said. He was still very pissed.

Omar couldn't take his two pills and talk at the same time. First things being first, his eyes seemed to go blank as he chased them down with his bourbon. "We haven't even met one long-legged bitch yet." He was drooling, but still trying to shake himself into focus.

Mickey leaned over to Charles. "He's fucked up. You gotta ignore his shit."

Charles heard him. He didn't look away from his beer. Harry and Butch heard him too. Omar couldn't possibly hear anything.

"Charles," Mickey said.

Charles's lips moved a little.

"Charles," he said again.

This time there was contact with Mickey's chin.

"You sure that wasn't the mail you lost?"

Charles didn't hesitate one second too much. "Yes sir."

Butch heard and said something. Mickey had to yell at him to repeat it. He still didn't hear, and Butch, about as loud as someone with a normal voice, shouted, "Secret agent mail, ya me dijo!" Which caused lots of heads to turn back to the interesting conversations at their own table.

Harry, whose body talk said it was time to go, was saved when the band took the stage. "We finally get music," he sighed to Mickey.

They were three guys, on lead, bass, and drums, and a woman singer. Only one of the guys didn't wear a Stetson. He wore a bandanna instead and no shirt. The woman singer wore a frilled leather skirt, and they all wore western boots.

They mixed it up. Early rock 'n' roll and country, some swing, some harder, younger rock. It made for some good dancing, and lots of people in the club used the floor in front of the band, maybe even too many, because a couple of guys suddenly got into it and started throwing blows. The band stopped and bouncers, white boys as huge as any TV-star Texans, came and busted it up, driving both offenders to and out the swinging front doors.

Harry, practically cheering the occasion, tried to talk across the table to Mickey, over the band, which had gone back to its duty.

"I can't believe this! Now I know it's Texas!"

"It's El Paso, the Wild West," Mickey corrected him. Mickey was now the only one left to speak to him. Butch and Charles didn't count, and Omar'd disappeared, leaving behind his body. "Lotsa tough hombres and badass cabrones," Mickey said, staring at Omar.

"Nobody'll believe me," Harry exulted.

"You won't forget this cowboy show, that's for sure."

Omar groaned back to life and unslumped himself from his chair. It seemed to occur to both Mickey and Harry at the very same instant how suddenly comic Omar'd become. His ridiculous clothes stuck on him like some black-humor pasties, his hairy belly had popped the buttons that kept it from getting its needed scratching, his tie was noosed over his back. And then, as each of them began independently to chuckle over how much that meant anything or not, Omar—in a thundering voice so original that no one ever would be able to imitate or describe it, so electric that everyone, every single person, employees and patrons, dancers and sitters, drinkers and band members, froze like lightning had sucked out all other power—arched his head up toward the beamed ceiling, shut his eyes, and cut loose, syllable by syllable: "LUCY! YOU FUCKING BITCH! YOU FUCKING WHORE! LUCY, WHERE ARE YOU?! LUCY! LUCY, WHO THE FUCK ARE YOU FUCKING NOW!"

Omar didn't just throw up once but twice. And he wasn't private about it, but as spectacular as he was voluminous.

The Baby Huey bouncers didn't ask Mickey or Butch or Charles or Harry to leave on their way to pushing and dragging Omar out, they just expected it. But none of them resisted leaving, and since Omar didn't notice how degraded he was, none raised an objection about his treatment even if one had been offended on his behalf. Omar's head, his jaw muscles too weak to keep the lower mandible up, his tongue dangling at the corner of his wide-open mouth, fit snugly into the corner between the door and seat in the back of the Nova, right behind Harry, who was up front riding shotgun to Butch, who was driving. Harry, more surprised than anything else to have gotten out of the nightclub uninjured, didn't seem to have any trouble hearing Butch.

Charles, pinned between Mickey and Omar, had started mumbling to himself just enough that his lips would part, for sibilants to spit through his teeth. Mickey spent time trying to communicate or at least declassify before he gave up on it, which was when he realized he too could hear every word Butch was saying. This was just about as astonishing as Omar's outburst, and even more so since the wind, blowing stiff and wild and straight

into them, was a flooding river of air—aluminum and tin cans,
paper and cardboard boxes swooping upon the windshield like
rocks or even boulders, a black plastic garbage bag rolling over and
under along the road like a body, its rubbish flesh still alive and
suffering—that challenged Butch's voice, and lost.

"I haven't been home," Butch was telling Harry, "since I
went outta the pinta, you know, the joint. Because my old lady,
my wife, she stopped visiting me when I got over at La Tuna, when
I got transferred down, right here a few miles away. Well, you
know, you get used to being alone. And, you know, I been here,
not doing ni madre, not nothing. And, pues, now that Omar gived
me these wheels, I guess I am gonna go on back. I decided, and,
well you know, I'm gonna see. Probably she got some other viejo
now, you know. I understand. Es lo que, it's what happens, ya
sabes. What can you do? Or why, you know? But I'm gonna go
back porque I got three kids, and they're all bigger now, y tal vez
they don't even know who the fuck I am ahora. But they are still
all little chavalos, maybe the oldest she is ten or so, and the
youngest, he's maybe seven now. I went to the store, and I bought
them juguetes, some toys, I didn't know what to get or what they
want, but I took my paycheck and bought them the toys. And then
I got something for my old lady, maybe I give it to her, you know,
I don't know, if, pues, ya sabes. It's a toaster because it's a joke.
She want a toaster, and we didn't have no toaster, and before I got
into the joint, before all that pedo came down, I told her I was
gonna get her a toaster. I put it all in the trunk, and I'm gonna go
there, gonna drive out there. Who knows, you know?"

Butch was driving to the top of the mountain for tourist
purposes. With Omar passed out and snoring, and Charles behind
them, the visor of his cap aimed downward, shading his sight from
something not glary to anyone but him. Harry, assured that it was
the last stop before the Wild West bedtime, acted easier with

Omar passed out and snoring, and he practiced Spanish phrases
with Butch as they'd wound up the road and parked it, and when
the two of them got out of the car and touched their knees into
the rock guard rail on the cliff side of the road, talking and talking
like Mickey'd never heard out of Butch before.

Mickey made himself invisible downhill from the car and
took off into darkness, away from voices. Nothing was unintentional. Not the star-punctured sky, the bleached moon, not the
blackened earth below: a gulf of flat desert ringing to the curved
brim, falling into the emptiness of this world. Except the emptiness wasn't really at that faraway edge. The emptiness was all
around, and the moon, suspended in it precariously, perilously,
was evidence and proof, night after night. Those lights below—
window lights, streetlights, head- and taillights—were broken
glass, shards and slivers and chunks moonlit to sparkle yellow and
white and green and red and blue, the remains of bottles from a
celebration still going on, and they'd been tossed against this
mountain. It was a good party, fun. People drank, and some drank
too much. They laughed and argued. Men and women fell in love,
made love, fought against and for. Maybe the stupid ones cracked
the bottles against the rocks. Or it was their kids who did. Little
kids liked the echo of the glass spilling into the rock, liked the
explosion of color. The broken pieces became gems to be found
later by even younger kids hunting around for some stones that
weren't always gray or brown. Red would be the best. Or yellow.
That gold was easy enough to see from the height on the mountain,
where, from up here, it was spread around plentifully, and was
beautiful to stare at, and to hope for.

Right then, he'd say, he decided.

*   *   *

It was Isabel, the maid.

Mickey opened the door without hesitation. He didn't look around. He didn't think a thing, maybe because he'd just walked in a few hours earlier and hadn't slept. A long walk from the top of the mountain.

"How are you?" she asked.

Was she smiling at him in a friendly manner? "Fine, fine, how are you?"

"Very good," she said. Was she being bashful, shy?

"I think I'll go take a shower," Mickey told her. He wished he had some clean clothes. He hadn't washed anything in at least a month.

She'd noticed. "Do you want me to wash them for you?"

"You could do that?"

"At my house. I can bring it all back after."

"That would be, well, tremendous. Good, you know."

She still giggled at his use of the word "tremendous."

Together they heard the man in the room across the hall cut one. She averted her eyes and grinned, shaking her head.

Mickey, for the first time, wasn't ashamed, didn't feel like he'd been the one with the farts. He laughed, guiltless, too.

"Should I just leave them here? In a pile?"

"I'll pick them up later."

"Well then, I'll go, I'll go take a shower."

She looked embarrassed by the idea. Didn't she? The possibility made Mickey feel better. "Okay, then. Thanks." He strutted down the hall.

That same morning Isabel found Mr. Crockett in his room. Gossip contended that he'd been dead for days. He'd sunken forward in the common—in every room—desk chair, facing the high window, his white-tipped cane between his legs. An ambulance arrived and its uniformed men carried the corpse, draped by an unadorned, clean, ironed white sheet, into the back hatch of the modified automobile.

The Sarge served, more determined each time and never less, no matter how weak his previous serve was, until he got it right. Mickey lost the first game 21–18.

Mickey was wiped out from the night before because he hadn't gotten any sleep yet, though he might have argued, if he really wanted to get out of it, how it was out of respect for Mr. Crockett's death. The court was reserved, and it was the hour they'd always played except that one day when Mickey missed. The Sarge believed religiously in the routine, and it had been at his insistence.

"You know," Mickey said, "maybe this isn't the best day for this."

The Sarge spun away, too galled to speak.

"Never mind," Mickey said, not ambitious enough to fight with words. "I forgot how *important* this is."

"Are you saying you're not going to try?"

"I'm gonna whip your fucking ass, Elias. Get ready."

Mickey served and won 21–14 and it wasn't that close.

The Sarge, a drink of water and a wipe of a towel later, opened the match game. He served perfect lobs one after another into the corner, skimming the wall on Mickey's left hand, until a lucky kill-shot return ended the run—he came away up, 7–0.

In the past, Mickey only had to concentrate, play a more deliberate defense until Sarge's surge deflated. But this time he kept returning Mickey's serve and it was Mickey who was running around the floor, from corner to corner, in a sweat. The Sarge held the position in the center of the court, in absolute charge.

Mickey's intention—he never denied it—was to win, and he made it a fight, and trailed by as close as one, but he couldn't overcome the early lead the Sarge had taken. The Sarge had played his best game, 21–16.

Mickey shook his hand.

"Finally!" the Sarge cried out. "I cannot believe how hard that was! I thought you might never lose!" The Sarge made a fist out of one hand and it pounded the air involuntarily. Though not exactly gloating, his pleasure wasn't to be misunderstood. This hadn't been just any old match for him. Much like Charles when he lost, the Sarge dove into a private world of significance. He *beat* Mickey, he overcame a bad metaphor.

In the coffee shop, the Sarge, exhausted, still wheezed more oxygen into his lungs.

"Here you go, hone-neys," Lola said. "If the coffee is not hot and good, you just tell Lola, and I fix her up." She winked familiarly at the Sarge. "Is this all you big mens are gonna have?"

"The number three breakfast," said the Sarge. "For both of us. I finally took down this brat today, and I'm buying him breakfast."

"Que bueno!" Lola exclaimed. "Por fin!"

Lola knew too much. Mickey read the sign and felt the grin. "You been seeing her, huh, Sarge?"

The Sarge shook his head, but not to refute Mickey's insight.

"Come on, boss, own up!"

He nodded, modest or ashamed.

"You dog!" Mickey wanted so much to recall, out loud, when was the last time he'd heard the metal bed banging the plaster, but that kind of cruelty wasn't there, not even this day. He didn't feel like knocking his neighbor off.

The Sarge sipped his hot coffee. The man from Michigan floated like a hawk.

"Well," Mickey said, so relieved that his doubt about the Sarge was over, "it don't matter, I'm proud of you."

Fred was frowning, which meant he was seriously bothered. An obese man thumped the edge of the desk counter with a Bible covered by imitation red leather, his free hand flicked at a short red tie the texture of a potato sack. It was a rhythm he timed well and practiced often. Excessive in more than just his fat—the lapels of his beige suit were the width of poncho flaps, and the fresh red carnation in his left buttonhole was as heavy as a baseball—his voice wasn't so much high volume as potent. "I'd hate to provoke the wrath of Almighty God," he told Fred, "but if I hafta bring in the law, so be it."

Fred had motioned for Mickey, who met him away from where the preacher man planted the breadth and length of his immense loafers, which maybe had never seen polish ever. "Do me and this gent here a favor and go check and see what's going on with him. He's supposed to have gone up to his room, but he hasn't come back."

"Who?" Mickey asked.

"Charles Towne," said Fred.

The preacher eased over, sweating profusely, wiping it away with his palm. That explained the motion to the tie—he used it as a towel. "Said he'd keep all them things up in his room and I thought that they'd be right fine since I thought he was a normal boy," he explained to Mickey. "Didn't suspect him wanting to skip out on me."

Fred told him about the items the preacher man claimed

Charles had for the church work they did together. "Says he found him at the bus depot this morning," Fred said.

"Did found him at the bus station," the preacher affirmed. " 'Gonna go to New Orleans,' he says. I took him by the arm and drug him back. Just luck, too, me being there. Can't understand why you won't let me just go up and get it. It's mine. What's mine is mine."

"Nonresidents are not allowed upstairs," Fred said. "How many times do I have to tell you?"

"Get my belongings returned if it takes getting the law, if that's what she takes."

Mickey carried a master key to Charles's room, knocked and called for him. He unlocked the door after he'd waited long enough, then went in. It was all there, just like the preacher said: amp and speakers, a microphone, a dictionary-sized Bible, and, in a cardboard box nearby, cheaply printed religious pamphlets. For example, one, in a bilingual printing, about God's Damned, made the claim that certain men, women, boys, and girls—these words were underlined—were made bad not because they had a preference for liquor or drugs or sex, but by God's decree. Were you one of God's damned? it asked, because Salvation was only by repentance through Jesus, the Lamb of God. Other than these statements, what struck Mickey was how unmelodramatic Charles's living circumstances were. It might have been for the simple reason that he had so little—three shirts hung in the closet below a hard, empty suitcase on a shelf above, a pair of tennis shoes were on the floor, and Omar's Juárez shirt was hooked on the edge of the closet door. In a drawer Mickey opened were boxer shorts, one pair of pants, the shorts and T-shirt he wore in the gym, and some dark socks rolled into balls, a toothbrush and toothpaste, a bar of soap in a plastic holder, hair shampoo, and plastic throwaway razors. In the drawer below was the gun, a small pistol, a .22 caliber, which might have been something to chew over if it weren't for what it was resting on: mail. The drawer was overstuffed with mail. Piles of used envelopes, stamped or metered, the majority slit cleanly on one side by a letter opener, but all completely empty of contents. They'd been dirtied and smeared and crumpled, stained with coffee and food and ashes, they were scribbled and doodled on—every one of them clearly liberated from trash, most likely from the dumpster in the back of the building. They had been collected, straightened out as much as possible, sorted and organized. On the bottom left-hand corner they'd been dated, each month hand-written in full, no abbreviations, sometimes in print, sometimes in longhand, with a day and year, evidently the day he dug them up. Except for a loose few at the top, the piles were rubber-banded, a month or two worth in some, more in others. All had been sent to the YMCA, but not all were envelopes from businesses, and some were addressed to residents.

"He's not in the room," he told Fred when he got back down. Mr. Fuller was standing there as well, his icy demeanor suggesting to Mickey that there wasn't approval of Mickey's doing the search of the room. "That stuff is in there, though. Didn't know if I should bring it or not."

"No," Fuller said firmly. He'd loosened his tie, and the jacket was unbuttoned. "I will not allow it to be given to this man unless Mr. Towne himself does it."

In the breast pocket of the preacher's suit, the caption from another pamphlet popped up like from the window of a cash register: WHO'S IN CONTROL? The preacher'd rested his Book on the desk and was tugging open a bag of cheese puffs, a fizzing diet soda in wait. "Well, I'd by God like to hear him deny they are not my belongings. We can call the law if that's what she takes."

"It won't do any good," Mr. Fuller told him again. "I won't allow anything to be removed from the room without his permission."

It came to Mickey and he was right: Charles was in the ping-pong room. Since it was still too early for the residents to play, the lights were off, and Charles was pacing, slumped, as substantial as the shadows, carrying on a multisyllabic dialogue with himself, brushing against the plastic rubber tree plant on each pass.

"What time is it?" he asked Mickey. He had seen Mickey come in, just not made one sign that he had. He was in his socks, which were too big and flapped under his toes, his hands were buried into baggy pants, stretching his suspenders.

Mickey guessed the approximate time. "Why?"

"It must be . . . ," Charles started. "It must be . . . in New Orleans . . ."

"What's going on, Charles? What's wrong?" Mickey'd say he was responsible for him suddenly wanting to run back to New Orleans. He was certain that the ping-pong game was what caused that.

Charles hadn't stopped talking to himself or pacing. "What time is it?" he asked Mickey again.

Mickey guessed the approximate time once more. "Charles, there's this big fat preacher who wants his stuff back. You know who I'm talking about?"

Charles didn't listen, and Mickey went on back to the front desk. "I found him," he told the three men there. He told them about the pacing and ongoing conversation.

The preacher bobbed his head in disbelief. "Can't understand it," he said, his lips and tongue yellow with synthetic cheese. "What you suppose gets into some kinda men?"

Mr. Fuller didn't like any of this, but mostly he didn't like

Mickey, even in this instance. At least that's how Mickey was picking up on it, since Fuller seemed truly sympathetic to Charles and didn't like Mickey's report. "We're gonna just leave him alone," he told Mickey. "He's got his rights."

"All I want is what's mine." The slob preacher crumpled up the empty bag of cheese puffs and dropped it next to the diet soda, where it crackled back into its original shape. He wiped his mouth with his palm and cleared his throat. "I got rights too. What's fair is we all go and see what the boy has to say about me getting my belongings returned to me." His hand was wiping his tie, and vice versa.

Mr. Fuller wasn't fond of the idea, but he followed along grudgingly, Mickey leading the way. Fred stayed behind at the desk.

Charles wasn't in the ping-pong room anymore.

"Now what?" Mr. Fuller said to both and neither of them.

The preacher shook his head in disbelief.

Fuller walked off, mad. Then he stopped and snarled back. "Come on," he told the preacher contemptuously. "I'll see you to the door."

"I'll get me the law if I have to."

"You go ahead," Fuller told him. "You call the police right after you've left here."

Mickey visited the men's room. First he heard Charles in there, then saw his stocking feet beneath a stall door. "Charles," he said as he faced the urinal and emptied his bladder.

Charles quit talking to himself.

"Charles, whadaya think you wanna do? You know, about that stuff the preacher wants back."

"Same thing I did yesterday," he said after a long pause.

Mickey was encouraged. "Well, okay. So wha'd you do yesterday?"

"I don't know," said Charles carefully.

Mickey could almost laugh. "Makes sense to me," he told him. "It really does make perfect sense." He zipped up his pants and left.

Mickey didn't find Omar in his room—he wasn't sure why he went to see him. Maybe just to be happy about his hangover. He was passing by Butch's room.

"So Omar's buddies checked out?" he asked, making a seat out of the edge of this room's desk.

Butch lay on his back on the bed, a mostly empty quart of beer next to him. Mickey couldn't help being himself. He took off on the story about Charles, until, that is, he caught on that Butch didn't give a shit. Or worse, that Butch didn't give a shit about any Mickey story. That's how he read it. And so he got up to leave when he heard Butch say something.

"What?" Now Mickey had no patience for trying to hear this guy.

"You seen pinche Omar?" Butch said.

"No."

Butch again said something that Mickey couldn't make out, and Mickey was willing to leave it at that. "How come I could fucking hear you so good last night, man?"

"Aquel pinche culero took off in the car," Butch said, speaking up. "All that shit I gots for my babies and my old lady. I got it all in the trunk, bro. I know the fucker ain't coming back neither."

"Maybe he's out with his compañeros."

"Cuáles?"

"Those dudes. You know."

Butch didn't.

"That guy last night, he was one of them," Mickey said. "You know who I'm talking about."

"No ways."

"Why you saying that?!" Mickey said, pissed off.

"Porque he don't know those dudes." Butch was barely audible.

"For sure he knows that one," Mickey said, loud. "You know, Harry, that went with us last night. *Harry*. He knew that guy from some place." He was genuinely upset. "Why would I think he knew him if he didn't?"

"No ways," Butch said, bitter, stretching his neck in bed. "Must be you think crazy, bro."

Mickey stopped himself from pulling Butch up to his feet by his T-shirt. "He knew him from before, I'm telling you! How come you're so sure?!"

Butch started talking too low again.

"I can't hear a fucking word you're saying! Talk like you did last night! I could hear you talking to that Harry!"

"That he don't know the dude," Butch said a little louder.

Mickey was beginning to remember when those guys checked in, but was resisting it too. "Sure he does!" He felt like he'd been sucker-punched. "Why would I fucking think that? How can you say he didn't know the dude from before?"

"Porque I was talking to him, like you said you heard me. He was a pinto como yo. But he don't know Omar, never did."

Lightheaded, Mickey stood up to leave. "Seemed like both you guys knew him. He said that as much for himself. I swore it. I swore."

"He just did time. Did time on the East Coast. Estaba en la mafia allí, me dijo." Butch swilled the last of the beer. "That pinche Omar took off with my babies' toys," he went on, just audibly.

* * *

Mickey ate more soft bread and soft cheese than usual, downed a lot more lukewarm water. His hunger nagged him because he ate breakfast with the Sarge, but he couldn't give into everything he felt. He couldn't figure out what else to do, so he tried the western.

This time Jake was saving Consuela from outlaw gringos he killed but who shot him in the process. A bullet had wedged itself in his ass, and Consuela had to dig it out of him. She giggled when he had to take off his pants for her. He didn't want to make a souvenir out of the bullet because he couldn't carry them all in his saddlebags, like she suggested. Not that many, she noticed. But an awful lot, she told him, examining the scars on his manly physique, impressed and awed. Then she couldn't control herself. He was too much for her to resist. And so, her hands all over him, Jake's wounds began not to feel so bad.

Mickey pitched the book toward the trash can—and sank it. Was he jealous? Maybe it was a little bit that. But mostly he was tired of this Jake doing so well. Tired of it going so smooth out in his Wild West, for him and everything he did being believable. He was tired of this woman being misnamed Consuela—the other beautiful Mexican women in the book, Consuela's sisters, were named Carmen and Magdalena—and falling for dipshit cowpokes that never had a dime either.

"You better take a quick peek at the schedule first," Fred told him. Oscar was leaning into his usual spot.

"I got a different day?" Mickey passed through the short swinging door and went to the wall behind the desk. "But I don't see my name."

Fred nodded.

Mickey sorted it out for a second or two. "So what's this mean?"

"There's a check here for you," Fred told him. He played indifferent about it. "You want me to cash it?"

"Fuck. That pussy can't say it to me himself or what?" Mickey finally acknowledged Oscar, who was watching him, waiting to see what the next event would be.

"He said you knew it wasn't a permanent position," said Fred.

"What's this *really* about, Fred?"

Fred shook his head, but not like he didn't know, only that he wouldn't say.

"I should pay a visit to that fucking pendejo." Mickey saw Mrs. Schweitz in the office, bent over her work, consumed, pretending to not hear, nothing to do with her. "So was this before or after that stuff with Charles Towne?"

"The schedule's been here since this morning."

"He already hired somebody else?"

"He was supposed to start but can't until tomorrow. That's what he told me. Fuller's doing the shift tonight himself." Fred smiled ironically. Then Fred shifted toward him, conspiratorially. "He won't be able to handle it either."

"Should I beat the shit out of him, Fred?"

Fred laughed uncomfortably. Oscar didn't even grin.

"Cash the check," Mickey said, coming around to the outside of the counter. He signed the note, and Fred counted out cash and change from the register. Mickey let his eyes rest in the direction of Mrs. Schweitz. "Was it her daughter? Or the other one, Mária?"

Fred hesitated. "He got a few complaints about you from a

few sources, but I think it was the girls.'' Fred didn't speak to
Mickey's face.

"Fuck him.'' Mickey moved toward the elevator doors and
waited patiently for them to open. He wanted it to appear that he
didn't really care, that he was in control.

Push-ups, sit-ups. He did as many as he could, until his
muscles would allow not one more, until he was so flushed he felt
feverish. It was dusk, the yellow curtain light mixing into the gray.
He had the window open. The wind pushed the curtains around
at will, causing the fabric to slap the halls, to pull at the metal rods,
helping the sky to jump through and right at him. He shut his eyes
because he was tired of it too.

He wanted to remember true and real things: The night
before, when he'd climbed down the mountain, hopped up and
down boulders, kicked loose rocks and broken glass, he saw how
the moonlight turned ice blue around the drooping street lamps
and under their hives of pale yellow—like the wind, the desert and
the mountain were still everywhere he walked. It was rocks and
dirt, and they were in walls and on streets and against the sidewalks and curbs. Rocks might be gathered and piled and sorted,
mixed and separated, they might be used for fences and founda-
tions and for walls of homes, but they were never under control,
never not kicked accidentally or thrown away, and the dirt, dug
up, piled, graded, watered, no matter what temporary domination
or management, won over most front and backyards, alleys, ease-
ments, and lots. The desert and the mountain were the ever-
present wilderness in these neighborhoods of western gables, the
one- and two-story buildings with columned porches and balconies
of bowed, broken railings and floorboards and trim, the paint on

them sapped of juices, natural and man-made, no longer able to bond, peeling away, chipping, dropping like seed.

He'd found an old tennis ball and, walking, bounced it on the sidewalk cracked by time and filled in by weeds—green, fertile young weeds that grew tall and were so mean that their leaves were crusty like a reptile, with dense, short, woolly spines that hadn't yet evolved enough to punish contact like a cholla cactus. He'd climbed over a chain-link fence and into an elementary school yard and tossed his tennis ball at the little windows of the little house on the wall—that was what he thought it was then and still too. He got in a stretch position and called strikes and balls. The smell of warm masa and burnt grease in the cold air, he sat on the asphalt at the cross of a four-square court, lobbing the ball at a set of cement stairs, remembering when he was still a boy, when he didn't know about much else. He rode horses. There were lots of birds: doves and mockingbirds, hawks and grackles, quail, owls. Dogs howled, cats brawled. Sometimes a coyote, sometimes a snake. Crickets and cicadas. He cried about thorns and needles and stings. There were fly balls and passes. He aimed a .22 rifle at a can, and he dreamed of adventure and fame.

Almost asleep, Mickey heard the Sarge whistling a happy, boring, and stupid tune, which he hadn't heard him do since they began playing handball together. The Sarge had finally won. The Sarge opened the door to his room and quit the cheerful puckering as soon as he tuned into his muzak on the radio.

Then he heard Charles's voice outside the window. "Take it! You can have it all!" A crash. "I don't want ANY of it!" More came plummeting from the window. Charles, in a room directly below, was screaming incomprehensibly, throwing things against the walls beneath. Then more was heaved out the window. Then more screaming, more stomping. The Sarge's music went off—he was listening too. Eventually, after a while, the noise from Charles's room ended too.

Mickey couldn't get to sleep, and he really wanted to. So balls are bounced, passed, shot.

"Nobody wins every time, everybody knows that."

"But your streak died."

"If I'd lost once in the middle, you'd say how great it was I only lost once."

"Maybe so."

"No maybe about it."

"So you don't mind losing?"

" 'Course I mind."

"Some say you lost because you were sick or injured."

"I lost, no excuses. When you lose you want to feel like it was because something was wrong. But I've won when I've been sick or injured too."

"Then you think he's caught up with you?"

"Who can say? Time will tell. You know what, that question pisses me off. How come you even ask it? How come I can't just lose one or two like others? How come I have to account for it? People lose all the time and they don't have to say shit."

"You're upset about losing."

"No I'm not. I'm not. Look, just forget it, okay?"

It doesn't work anymore. Can't get sleep this way. He's got to go. He can't stay.

He falls asleep anyway. Or almost.

He remembered how he thought the light wasn't yellow after all. It was brown. Like dirt. He heard clicking, which was probably just his heart, a flap of muscle thrashing, but, afraid as he was, he stalked it before it got him first, approached as close as he could, and then BANG! the explosion whistled and burst like flesh and sinew and bone—it was death. Death was in him, and the color of the room, the brown, that was the soil dropping on him in shovelfuls. But still his imagination—he wasn't sure about what to name it—went with that exit wound—a bullet, in a western—and his mind, or whatever you called it, followed, or stuck, gummed it up, and that matter expanded until it became small, a small knot, something, which went on getting smaller, tunneling fast toward a light the shape of the sun.

Mickey forced himself awake and stayed alert a short time that seemed long. It had happened. He knew it. *Knew.* And he was still alive. This he was sure of, absolutely sure of. He could hear his breath and heart beating. This was true. There was a strangeness in this sensation of life: a joy that ached like sadness.

He wasn't sure how long someone had been knocking. It couldn't have been the Sarge because Mickey'd played handball the day before. And Isabel—she *had* forgotten to pick up his laundry; the pile of it was still on top of his desk. He got out of the bed and opened the door, shirtless and barefoot. Had he slept at all? "Come on in," he told Butch. He yawned and stretched. "What a night. Slept like shit."

"So you been in here?" he asked like he didn't believe. Butch talked as loud, and excited, as he did that night.

"Where else?"

Butch wasn't making eye contact. "I dunno, bro."

"I'm outta here," Mickey told him. "Fuck it."

"You didn't do it?" Butch was looking at him straight. "I thought maybe you did it, 'cuz I heared the vato fired you, and . . ."

"He was too pussy to fire me. He couldn't say it to my face."

Now Butch looked away. "Entonces, no lo hiciste. Es que, you say you didn't do it?"

"Do what? What the fuck you talking about?"

"Que Big Ears got blown away." He waited on Mickey. "I bet lots of the guys are saying you did it."

Mickey carefully reviewed the information to himself.

Butch listened, but Mickey didn't make a sound. "Anoche, at the end of your shift. They got Charles, cuffed him y todo. Pero, the way we heared it, fue como un hit. Había un balazo aquí"— Butch rubbed three fingers between his eyebrows—"y otro acá," palming between the pectorals. He gave that a couple of seconds to set up. "La cosa es que, I was thinking, you know, about what you told us, me and Omar, y también lo que el me dijo una vez, que, like, ya sabes, he didn't really believe you, pero, but that you were the type, he said, that went off, como aquel loco, that crazy fucker."

"Like who?" Mickey tried to think. "You mean the Reverend Miller?"

Butch nodded and smiled at Mickey and through him. "I didn't tell nobody, you know, what Omar said. I don't think he was right."

"Fuck him. Omar's a fucking asshole." Offended at Omar's comparison, Mickey took a few more seconds before he went back to the other. "I was here." He picked out a white shirt, one like he always wore, and began buttoning it.

Butch said something Mickey couldn't understand.

"I couldn't hear you. What?"

This time Butch seemed to not want anyone else to hear. "Entonces, it wasn't that other thing you was telling us about?"

"Which?" Mickey pulled on socks, then over them his boots. "You mean that shit about the mail?"

Butch nodded, eyes right into Mickey's. "It's 'cuz, those vatos, those dudes were bad, from the East Coast, like you always said."

Mickey started stuffing his duffel bag.

"Y es más . . . ," Butch shortened the space between them, whispered below his normal low, ". . . that some of the dudes here, they say they saw the other vato, con la boina, the beret, just before. That he was around . . ."

Mickey interrupted. "Wait. Don't think it, okay? It's not what happened. It didn't have nothing to do with me. Anyways, I said the West Coast, not the fucking East Coast."

Butch nodded, making eye contact with everything except Mickey.

Butch didn't believe him. Because this was exactly what someone would say if he were lying. *Exactly* what he would have to say. The only smart answer. Mickey had called it before, he was right, and now he had to deny it, didn't he?

"So they think it was Charles?" Mickey asked.

Butch nodded and smiled at him.

Butch and Mickey took the elevator down without talking. Mickey was expecting more when they stepped out. He couldn't believe how everything in the lobby seemed the same. Fred was behind the desk, and Oscar was leaning against the counter, though not with the usual angle. He was more erect, his body not relaxed against the rim of the counter.

John Hooper rounded the corner from the coffee shop, a toothpick in his mouth. He stopped for Mickey. "Another day with the nuts and homos and God knows what," he said, thumbing his cowboy hat upward. "I thought for sure it was that crazy reverend." He folded his arms and shook his head, disgusted with the place. "I'm here, I keep my door shut." His boots clacked over to the elevator, he pushed the UP button, and the doors parted. Once John Hooper was inside, the doors shut again.

"So they're sure it was Charles Towne?" Mickey asked Fred. Mrs. Schweitz wasn't in.

Fred tightened his eyebrows and nodded.

"They say why?"

Fred didn't answer quickly. "The mail. They're saying it was about the mail."

Oscar tilted his head at Mickey like he'd finally figured out who Mickey reminded him of.

"The mail," Mickey repeated.

Fred gazed off nowhere in particular.

Butch was right behind Mickey.

"Doesn't make sense," Mickey said. "I can't see Charles doing it."

"The dude with the beret fingered him," Butch said barely loud enough, smirking.

"Is that true?" Mickey asked Fred.

Fred nodded. "It's what I hear."

Butch stared at Mickey like he wanted to wink. He was convinced.

"It was his gun, though, right? They got Charles with the gun?"

"I guess so," Fred said. It was as though Fred didn't know Mickey anymore. Like Mickey had only been a resident all this time. "I'm not the police. You'd have to ask them."

Before he checked out, Mickey decided to take one last swim. He'd been getting better; he could swim a half a mile without stopping, then another. Most, though not all, of the regular old guys, in their goggles and masks and snorkels and skintights, were steadily kicking and stroking, going and going. Like nothing had happened. Mickey shared half a lane, fit his plastic goggles over his eyes, pushed off, let himself dissolve into the muteness of the water. Back and forth. Then he saw the Sarge get in next to him, and after several laps, he still felt the Sarge swimming a body length behind. Mickey swam until suddenly he couldn't take it, this competition, this game. So he quit, lifting himself out of the pale blue water.

The Sarge came into the shower after Mickey. "You know what I'm hearing?"

Mickey shook his head.

"That it had something to do with you."

Mickey shook his head.

"It's stupid," said the Sarge. "The man went crazy. They found the gun in his room." The Sarge laughed. Since Mickey'd lost that handball game, Mickey didn't have the power over him anymore, and the Sarge spoke with authority again. "Another stupid story from these guys. Really it's your buddy Butch who's getting it going, telling everybody that it was supposed to be you, that it was a case of mistaken identity."

Mickey didn't say anything.

"So we're playing handball tomorrow?" the Sarge asked.

"I'm not sure," Mickey lied. "I'll let you know."

The Sarge smiled sarcastically.

"Wasn't Fuller a friend of yours?" Mickey asked him accusingly.

"I knew him better a long time ago. It's sad for his family. Real sad."

Mickey never did like this guy, and, he'd say, that was always one of his problems, guys like this.

"Hey," the Sarge said. "Just get a job, you know?"

Mickey nodded. "Oil the bedsprings," he said.

Back in room 412, Mickey finished stuffing his clothes in the duffel bag, glanced around, and shut the door just as the old man from across the hall—carrying a new and empty piss jar, gliding his socks on the glossy linoleum in his boxers and thinly woven, wide-necked T-shirt—arrived at his door after a visit to the toilet.

"Qué pasó?" he asked Mickey, proud of himself for speaking Spanish and being friendly. He was grateful.

"I'm okay. How you doing?"

"I'm okay too," he said. He didn't take notice of the bag on Mickey's shoulder. He smiled.

"It's good to hear," said Mickey. "I gotta go. See you later."

"Okay, hasta luego, I'll see you later," the old man said, and he crossed back into his room, turned up the volume on his TV set, and got back into bed.

"I'm booking out," Mickey told Fred. Oscar was there too. Mickey dropped the key to room 412 on the desk counter. "You boys be good now." The two men didn't smile or move.

He stopped at the door with Butch. "I can't believe that fucking Omar took all your shit," he said. Mickey did want, still, this minor victory: Omar wasn't right. Omar was an asshole.

"It was the bad shit," Butch said, back in his whisper voice, but also to be intimate. "You know, like you was telling us. Porque, it was como nos dijiste. Only the wrong desk clerk. He fucked up. They just put it on Charles." He wanted Mickey to tell him the true story.

Mickey shook his head. "I don't think so," he said.

Beside the double doors, where Mr. Crockett would be sitting, he made the dark glasses comfortable on the bridge of his nose.

Mickey had become sure he was alive, body and mind. And he was sorry—because it wasn't fair. It wasn't Fuller's fault. Wasn't Omar's or Charles's. He'd say it wasn't his fault either, but that he felt like it was. If, or only if. But no, *no,* it was not intentional, that, he now knew, was not true. *Knew.*

"Say good-bye to Isabel for me," he told Butch as he opened the double doors. He shook his hand. "Well, nos vemos, take it easy."

"A dónde vas?" Butch asked.

The light outdoors was white, the air blue, the sun yellow. It was a warm day in the West. Mickey wanted to walk. "I'm thinking I'll go across and see if I can stay with Ema a few days. Then, well, who knows?"

Yards away from the clear doors of the YMCA, Mickey played more with the fit of his dark mirror glasses. He moved unsteadily for a few steps as he balanced the weight of the duffel bag to his back. He walked a few blocks and waited on a red light. He crossed on the green and headed south, the direction of downtown, or the border.